DOOM MAGNET

THE LAST PICKS BOOK 3

GREGORY ASHE

H&B

Doom Magnet
Copyright © 2024 Gregory Ashe

Published by Hodgkin & Blount
https://www.hodgkinandblount.com/
contact@hodgkinandblount.com

Published 2024
Printed in the United States of America

Version 1.04

Trade Paperback ISBN: 978-1-63621-084-1
eBook ISBN: 978-1-63621-083-4

CHAPTER 1

"Bobby!" Millie screamed. "Over HERE!"

"Okay," Fox said. "I don't think now is the time—"

"Keme! Keme! Look! *Hi!*"

"Millie," Indira said, "they need to concentrate."

Torn between distracting her friends and, well, the thrill of simultaneously cheering/screaming at them, Millie settled for hopping up and down silently, waving her arms.

It was a bright October day, the weekend before Halloween. The sky was blue. The sun was warm. And although it was cooler than the summer months in Hastings Rock, on a day like today, you couldn't really tell.

Ketling Beach was a long, wave-smoothed crescent. To the north, Klikamuks Head jutted out into the sea. South, the shoreline curved inward, and across the bay rose the dollhouse profile of Hastings Rock. Where the light caught the wet sand of the beach at exactly the right angle, it looked sheeted in silver.

Banners hung everywhere, announcing the GREMLINS AND GROMMETS SURF CHALLENGE. In smaller type, the banners explained, *Brought to you by Gremlins and Grommets Surf Camp.* The event had brought out what looked like most of the town, and people lined the beach in folding chairs, many of them wrapped in blankets and carrying thermoses of coffee. Not exactly your Malibu beach scene, but I had learned—to my surprise—that not only did the Oregon Coast have some great surfing spots, the best time of year was late October. Which seemed like a wonderful recipe for death by hypothermia.

But if the cold water had deterred anyone, you couldn't tell by the number of surfers waiting to compete. Beyond the barrier that marked the end of the spectator zone, they ran the gamut from children with foamboards (presumably the gremlins and grommets, although I wasn't entirely sure of the lingo) to middle-aged men and women who looked scarily fit for their age. (This from a guy who prefers an elevator to stairs even when he's going down.)

Deputy Bobby and Keme were down there too. They were both wearing wetsuits as they did some light cardio, warming up for the day's events. If I had to make a list of terrible, awful, horrible ways to spend the day, watching Deputy Bobby jog and do jumping jacks and laugh at something Keme said probably wouldn't rank high on the list. It might not even make the list at all.

Although, to be fair, sitting next to Deputy Bobby's boyfriend, West, probably *would* make the list. In part, because I was doubly self-conscious every time I looked at Deputy Bobby. (Not that I was doing anything wrong. Not that I couldn't look at him. Because we were friends, right? And friends looked at each other all the time. Even when friends were in wetsuits, and you could see all their muscles, and friends were bending and stretching and—we're just friends!) And in part, because the juxtaposition wasn't ideal. I mean, West was gorgeous. He had flaxen hair in a messy part, perfectly pink cheeks, kissably pouty lips (at least, I assumed Deputy Bobby thought they were kissable), and eyes the exact same color as the sky this morning. He was wearing a ring on his left hand these days, so I guess I needed to start thinking of him as Deputy Bobby's fiancé. In keeping with the Halloween theme, he'd chosen to go as a very, very, very (need I go on?) sexy construction worker: hardhat rakishly cocked, hi-vis vest, jean shorts, steel-toed boots. And that, ladies and gentlemen, was all. If it were me, I would have been freezing, but since West also apparently had the metabolism of a hummingbird, he looked perfectly comfortable.

Everyone was dressed up, not just West, although nobody else, as far as I could see, had gone for the pouty-sexy-where's-my-metal-clipboard look, which should have been ridiculous, but honestly? He was totally pulling it off. Indira, of course, had kept her costume tasteful. I'd asked if she was going to be a witch, and she'd asked me why I thought that, and I'd immediately regretted every life choice I'd ever made. (Answer: it's because of that lock of white hair she has, which gives some seriously witchy vibes.) Instead, she'd gone for a tweed jacket over a rust-colored sweater and jeans, which looked like a normal outfit for her. She'd added big glasses and a crumpled deerstalker cap that sat cockeyed on her head, and when I'd finally had to ask who she was, she'd said Professor Trelawney. (Which, point for me because I had totally guessed witch.)

With Fox, it was hard to tell if it was a costume or daily wear, since Fox's outfits seemed to straddle the delicate intersection of Victorian train conductor, circus impresario, mortician, and steampunk enthusiast. Today, for example, they were wearing a knee-length frock coat over a Led Zeppelin tee, plus a top hat. (Hats were apparently a thing this Halloween.) Like I said, it was hard to tell if this outfit had been plucked from Fox's daily rotation or was a Halloween treat.

Millie, on the other hand, was definitely in costume. Millie's usual attire (which consisted of cute sweaters and jeans) had been replaced by a full '80s exercise getup: a neon pink leotard, turquoise tights, and electric yellow legwarmers and sweatbands. She'd done a full blowout on her hair and looked a little like Farrah Fawcett if she'd been struck by lightning. God bless her, she'd even found ankle weights. And the thing was…Millie looked amazing. I wasn't sure she even knew how good she looked because, well, she was Millie. But I knew one thing: I was dying to see Keme's face when the poor boy finally got a look at her.

As for me, I'd gone with something that I thought was clever. As usual, my friends had managed to blow up my expectations in a way that was both loving and devastating.

"I still don't get it," Fox said. "Are you a sex kitten?"

They chose the exact moment when I was drinking some of Indira's hot chocolate, which meant all I could do for several minutes was choke.

West glanced over at me, gave me an appraising look, and said, "Dominatrix-cat."

"Oh my God," Fox said. "That's exactly it."

"It's hot," West told me. "You're totally going home with someone tonight."

"No," I managed to wheeze through death-by-hot-chocolate.

"What is a dominatrix-cat?" Indira asked.

"I'll look it up," Millie announced.

"No!" Fox and I managed at the same time.

"Aren't you just a black cat?" Millie asked. "I thought the keys just got stuck to you like that time you got wrapped up in all that tape in your office and you couldn't get it off and you kept shouting for somebody to come help and Keme laughed and took all those pictures."

"This is not like that!" I took a deep breath, which was hard since I was still recovering from my near-death experience. "And I would have been fine except Keme kept making it worse—"

"Well, what are you?" Indira asked. "Why don't you just tell us?"

"Because this costume is clever and original and—and insightful."

"Insightful?" Fox murmured.

"And I'm not going to demean myself and demean you and demean the whole human race—"

"He gets on that high horse quick," West said, "doesn't he?"

"You have no idea," Fox said.

"—by explaining it," I finished. "And why are you all so focused on me? This is about Deputy Bobby and Keme." I fought with myself, lost, and added, "And nobody even asked Fox about their costume."

"I'm a polymorphed dragon," Fox said—a tad haughtily, in my opinion.

No one seemed to know what to say to that.

Indira recovered first. "West, I've got thermoses here with more hot chocolate and coffee, depending on what the boys want. I brought blankets. And I've got dry clothes. Is there anything else they need for when they get out of the water?"

Shaking his head, West said, "That's perfect. What they really need is to go home, get in a hot shower, and eat something, but you need a crowbar to get Bobby away from his board, even at the end of the day."

"Babe," Deputy Bobby called from the barrier to the spectator zone. He had his wetsuit rolled down to his waist, and God help me, I looked. The world froze. Angels sang. Trumpets, uh, blew—it sounded better in my head. He made an impatient gesture, and for a disoriented heartbeat, I started to rise.

"Let me guess," West said as he got to his feet. "Zipper's stuck."

"Keme tried, but he can't get it."

West slipped under the barrier and moved behind Deputy Bobby to inspect the wetsuit's zipper. Meanwhile, Fox asked in a breathy whisper, "Good God, how much time does Deputy Delectable spend in the gym?"

"At least an hour every day," I said automatically—because ninety-nine percent of my brain was trying to commit every inch of Deputy Bobby to memory and, at the same time, pretend like I wasn't looking. "Usually before work, but some days he has to go after."

"Is that so?" Fox asked, and they turned a curious look on me.

The note in their voice made me flush, and I probably would have stammered something that made everything worse, but fortunately, Keme came to my rescue. He was jogging toward us, his dark hair up in a bun, and his face was alight with excitement.

"Keme!" Millie shouted and waved.

That poor, poor boy.

The word poleaxed comes to mind. I saw the instant he caught sight of Millie. And then it seemed like he couldn't see anything else. His eyes were locked on her (Millie was still waving, obviously), and Keme began to veer off course.

"Uh, Keme," I tried.

"Keme!" Indira shouted.

Fox stood and bellowed, "Hey!"

None of it helped, though. He couldn't hear us. And so he jogged straight into a rack of surfboards.

Keme went down.

The surfboards went down.

Lots of people started yelling.

"Oh my God," Millie said. "Keme, I'm coming!"

"You know what?" Fox said. "He might be embarrassed. Let him get himself together first."

Millie didn't look happy about that, but she stayed. Keme got himself upright, seemed to shake off the daze—although I noticed that he was careful not to look in our direction again, which was probably a mixture of caution and embarrassment. He got the rack upright and started returning the surfboards to their places. Other surfers joined him, but the initial shouting had died down, and it looked like everyone was in good enough spirits that the accident turned into something to laugh about, rather than cause for a genuine argument.

"There you go," West said. "All set."

Sure enough, Deputy Bobby had his wetsuit zipped up now. In case you're wondering, it was actually kind of worse, somehow. I mean, it fit him like a glove, and that's all I'm saying. He gave West a kiss, and West squirmed away, laughing, before he said, "You're getting me wet!"

"What's there to get wet?" Fox asked *sotto voce*. "He's got about six inches of fabric on him total."

I shushed Fox.

"Are you ready, Bobby?" Indira asked.

Deputy Bobby wore that huge, goofy grin. "Water's perfect—do you see those swells coming in? Perfect breaks today."

"I assume that means it's all good."

"The lineup is going to take forever." But his tone made it clear this was a small objection. Then, in a different voice, he said, "Oh, come on."

Farther up the beach, a group of guys had paused halfway through putting up another beach tent. Even with the tent only partially erected, it was easy to read the words spray-painted in red on the fabric: THIEVES and TRESPASSERS.

"What's that about?" I asked.

"A protester," Millie said.

We all looked at her.

"Keme told me," she said.

"Her name is Ali Rivas," Deputy Bobby said, "and she claims every inch of this coast is sacred land for various Native American tribes. She's been raising a ruckus for weeks. Vandalism, destruction of property, threats. Jen calls in something new almost every day, but nobody can prove this woman, Ali, is doing it."

"She strikes again," Fox said, eyeing the graffitied tent that the men were now in the process of taking down.

"Is this really sacred land?" I asked.

Millie shook her head. "Some of the tribes used to fish here, of course, but the only nearby ceremonial sites and burial grounds are on the headland."

We all looked at her. Again.

"Keme told me," she repeated, this time with a laugh. "And anyway, the Confederated Tribes are sponsoring the competition—they've got a tent down that way."

"That doesn't make any difference to her," Deputy Bobby said. "She said the leaders of the Confederated Tribes were sellouts."

"Yikes," Fox said.

Another man, accompanied by deputies, walked over to the vandalized tent. He was average height, heavyset, dressed in a polo and pleated khakis, and his hair and goatee were black as coal. It was hard to tell at a distance, but I thought maybe he was older—something about the way he moved. He said something to the deputies, who in turn said something to the men, who let the tent fall. The deputies spread the tent flat on the sand, clearly preparing to take pictures of the damage.

"Who's that?" Indira asked.

West dropped into his seat again. "Gerry Webb."

"How do you know that?" Deputy Bobby asked.

"Because he tried to pick me up last night," West answered. He adjusted the hardhat and gave a rakish grin. "While you were in the restroom."

Deputy Bobby looked like he might be thinking a few words you wouldn't find in most dictionaries.

"He's a real estate developer," West continued. "And he must be a good one, because the watch he was wearing cost over a hundred thousand dollars."

"He's the one that's building the planned community on the other side of Klikamuks," Millie said. "Do you know how much he's going to charge? A million dollars for a house. And that's not even one of the houses on the waterfront. And they're going to have a marina and a bunch of new restaurants and—"

"Wait, a marina?" Fox squinted. "Isn't the surf camp on the other side of Klikamuks? Gremlins and Gruntlings, or whatever it's called?"

"Gremlins and Grommets," Deputy Bobby said drily. "And yes, that's where it is. I don't know the details, but Jen said she worked something out with him."

"Who's Jen?" I asked.

Before Deputy Bobby could answer, Keme trotted up.

"Oh my God, Keme, are you all right?" Millie scrambled over to inspect him. She stood close to him. She touched him. She was wearing perfume. And God help that poor boy, he was wearing a wetsuit.

I gave Deputy Bobby a telepathic nudge and a meaningful look.

He almost laughed. "He's fine, Millie. We've got to get in the lineup, or we're going to miss the best sets." With a slap to Keme's shoulder, he added, "Come on," and then he headed down toward the water.

Keme detached himself from Millie as gracefully as a seventeen-year-old boy can.

We settled into our seats, enjoying coffee and hot chocolate and cake (cranberry upside-down) and cookies (pumpkin cheesecake, which yes, can be turned into a cookie). The wind picked up again, stiff with the brine and carrying a hint of surf wax and what I thought might have been recreational, uh, substances. A fair portion of that seemed to be coming from Fox. Once Deputy Bobby and Keme had their boots and hoods on, they collected their boards. Keme's gear looked piecemeal—probably assembled from castoffs or whatever he'd been able to score cheap. Deputy Bobby's on the other hand, looked expensive. It made me think of the rotation of expensive sneakers he liked to wear—another layer in the enigma that was Deputy Bobby.

True to Deputy Bobby's prediction, there were a lot of surfers waiting in the lineup. But it was a beautiful day, and the waves were plentiful, and we watched (and Millie cheered) as Deputy Bobby and Keme slowly worked their way forward.

"I'm kind of sad we'll miss it," West said.

I glanced over.

"The new development," he said. "It sounds like exactly what Hastings Rock needs—a breath of fresh air, new money, new people."

Because Deputy Bobby and West were moving; that's what he didn't have to say. West had told me they were moving. It had been one of the first things he'd said after he and Deputy Bobby had gotten engaged. They were moving to Portland. They were moving away.

"Are you sure you can help load the truck next week?" West's question broke through my thoughts. "Bobby said you don't mind, but I know it's a pain—"

"No. I mean, yes. I mean, I'll be happy to help. Do you need help packing?"

"We're almost done, actually. Thank God I was able to talk Bobby into using his leave—can you believe he wanted to work right up until we left?"

I could, in fact. Because not only was Deputy Bobby very good at his job, but he also loved his job. It was part of who he was. Or maybe just who I thought he was. I had a hard time picturing him away from Hastings Rock. What would he do in Portland? Who would he be?

West's silence jarred a response out of me: "Fox said they'd help too—"

"Absolutely not," Fox said without looking up from their phone.

"I'll help," Millie said. "Dash, we could make it a RACE! And we could see how many boxes we can carry at one time. AND we could see who can pick up the heaviest box! West, are you sad you're moving? Are your parents sad? Are you going to miss Hastings Rock? We're going to miss you SO much! I'm probably going to cry when you and Bobby drive away. Oh my God, I think I'm going to cry right NOW!"

Indira patted her on the shoulder. "I already told Bobby I'll bring sandwiches and sweet tea. It's going to be a long day. And I'll pack you something for the road, too."

"It's only a couple of hours," West said with a smile, but he patted Millie's shoulder as she wiped her eyes. "Hey, don't cry. We'll come back to visit all the time."

Millie sniffled and nodded and said, "And we'll come visit YOU!"

Maybe it was the sudden ear-blast, but West didn't look quite so happy about that prospect.

I almost said, *You don't have to move, and then nobody will have to visit anybody*, but my phone buzzed (and my better judgment got hold of me). My dad's name appeared on the screen. (Jonny Dane, the Talon Maverick series.) A call from my dad was—well, unusual was putting it politely. My dad's focus was on my mom's books, on his books, and on his guns, and not necessarily in that order. I answered.

"Hey Dad."

"Hey, Dashiell. How's it going?"

"Uh, good. How are you?"

"Good, good. Listen, I've got a great opportunity. St. Martin's asked me to edit an anthology—crime fiction geared toward men, you know? And I thought it'd be perfect for you."

"For me?"

"How's that story going, the one with the PI?"

He meant Will Gower, a character who had lived in my head for as long as I could remember. (That sounded better than calling him my imaginary friend.) In various incarnations, Will Gower had been a hard-nosed police officer, a hard-nosed FBI profiler, and a hard-nosed private investigator. He'd also been a Victorian bobby, a social worker, and a deckhand on an Alaskan shrimping boat—you get the idea.

"Uh, good?"

"Great, great. Send it over. We've got to get moving on this."

"Well, it's not quite, um, ready. A hundred percent, I mean."

Dad was silent.

"It's almost done," I said. "It's so close."

Millie patted my shoulder. Fox snorted offensively. Indira started unpacking one of the slices of cake.

"I can finish it up?" It was a miserable-sounding question. "Next week?"

"Dashiell," he finally said—and it held an unbearable amount of parental long-suffering.

Fortunately, at that moment Deputy Bobby and Keme started paddling out to catch the next set.

"Dad, I've got to go. I'll get you the story next week."

As I disconnected, Millie screamed, "GO BOBBY! GO KEME!" And then, without missing a beat, "Dash, that's so exciting you're almost done with your story!"

Fox snorted again. For someone who was, themself, an artist (and one who—I'd like to point out—spent a high proportion of their artistic time lying on the floor, moaning about how they were a fraud and a grifter and an untalented hack), Fox gave surprisingly little leeway when it came to things like, uh, purposefully postponing the day-to-day instances of artistic production. (That sounded better than procrastinating by goofing off with Keme.)

"Here you are, dear," Indira said as she passed me the cake she'd been preparing.

It was a surprise cake (meaning I didn't even know she'd made it—the best kind), some sort of gingerbread confection. It was amazing, of course, and it went a long way toward taking the sting out of that conversation. My dad's silence. The way he'd said, *Dashiell*.

What helped more was that I got to watch Deputy Bobby catch his first wave. He made it look surprisingly easy when he popped up on his board, and even at that distance, I could see how natural he looked when he settled into his stance. He was actually kind of amazing—carving turns, slicing the water, his body leaning into each move until I was sure he'd fall. He didn't, though; he looked like he was glued to the board. I didn't know anything about surfing, but as far as I was concerned, it was incredible. And then, somehow, it got even better. Deputy Bobby launched himself off the lip of the wave. He went airborne, and as he flew above the water, he grabbed the back rail of the surfboard.

Millie screamed.

Fox shouted.

Indira shot to her feet, clapping.

West was jumping and waving his arms.

I was on my feet (I didn't remember that), bellowing Deputy Bobby's name.

It seemed like everybody else was cheering too, but I barely noticed. All my attention was on Deputy Bobby as he landed and rode the last of the wave toward shore.

And then it was Keme's turn. I recognized the look of furious concentration on Keme's face; every once in a while, I caught a glimpse of it when we were doing something else, when Keme forgot that he was supposed to be an unimpressed seventeen-year-old. His pop-up was a little less smooth than Deputy Bobby's, and it looked like he struggled, in the first few seconds, to keep himself upright. Then he caught his balance, and he seemed to change. The boy who vacillated between detached and surly (and occasionally outright combative) was gone, and in his place was a boy who looked…alive. That was the only word for it. It was like Keme was a house, and someone had turned on all the lights, and they were spilling out of him. He didn't have Deputy Bobby's finesse, not yet, but I thought, as I watched him carve the wave, that he might be more of a natural—if he kept surfing, he'd be better than Deputy Bobby one day; there was no doubt about that. But what made me grin until my face hurt was how happy Keme looked. How unselfconsciously at peace he seemed to be.

Like Deputy Bobby, he launched himself from the lip of the wave and caught air. Instead of reaching for the back rail of the board, though, Keme spun. He almost pulled it off, but as he was coming back around, he smacked face-first into the water.

"OH NO!" (Guess who that was?)

Fox winced.

"Oh my," Indira said.

"God." West held finger and thumb an inch apart. "He was so close."

I went for supportive (mostly because I knew it would both gratify and annoy Keme): "Great job, Keme! Good try!"

Keme surfaced and shook his head. He paddled back toward shore. Deputy Bobby was waiting for him at the halfway point, and when Keme came up beside him, Deputy Bobby said something. Keme shook his head again. Deputy Bobby stretched over to give Keme a one-armed hug. When they separated, they paddled the rest of the way together.

"Aww," Millie said.

Indira patted West's arm. "That's a very nice young man you found for yourself."

"Yeah," West said with a smile. "He really is."

"Hugs are boring," Fox said. "I want to see them fight!"

A voice came over the speaker system, announcing that they needed the surfers to leave the water for the under eighteen division. In ones and twos, the surfers started making their way back to shore.

"Wait," I said. "Keme isn't eighteen. Was he competing in the adult division?"

"Obviously," Fox said.

"How?"

"He lied about his age," Millie said. "He does it all the time. When we go to the theater in Seaside, he pretends to be twelve."

"Hold on. One time—once!—I asked him if he had his driver's license, and he wouldn't talk to me for a week. I mean, he never talks to me, but this was…icier."

"Movie tickets are expensive," Fox said with a shrug.

I looked at Indira.

"I've told him I don't like it," Indira said. "But when you add a drink and popcorn, sometimes it costs us fifty dollars."

"I don't care about the movie ticket! I care about the injustice of him getting mad at me—"

"Babe!" West screamed. He ducked under the barrier to sprint the remaining distance to Deputy Bobby, who was making his way up the beach with Keme. "You were amazing!"

Kissing ensued. Lots of kissing. And while Deputy Bobby was looking particularly, um, estimable, what with the wetsuit and the salt-stiff hair and the general, uh, effect, I decided to look elsewhere. Out of politeness.

"I guess West isn't worried about getting wet anymore," Fox said with unnecessary smugness. "You know, I think it's a little unfair that Deputy Delicious looks even better somehow after being in the water."

"Fox," Indira said in a warning voice.

"Dash looks handsome after he gets out of the water," Millie said—with dubious accuracy but heartwarming loyalty.

"Remember after we went swimming, when we went to get something to eat, and the waitress thought he was a drifter and said he could earn some money washing dishes?" Fox said and began to laugh.

Indira said a little more loudly this time: "Fox."

"That was not my fault!" I said. "You stole my towel, and—no! I'm not getting into this again!"

By that point, fortunately, Deputy Bobby and West and Keme had joined us. Indira was pouring cups of hot coffee, and Deputy Bobby and Keme were shivering as they took theirs.

"You were amazing," I told Deputy Bobby. And then I heard what I'd said, and I rushed to add, "You too, Keme."

Keme glowered at me over the rim of his cup.

"I could have done it better, though," I said.

For a heartbeat, the glower cracked, and a hint of a smile showed through. Then he went back to that flat stare.

"I definitely wouldn't have fallen. Remember that part? At the end?"

His glare slipped again, but only for a moment, and then he made a very rude gesture.

"God, that was so good," Deputy Bobby said. "It's perfect out there."

"One day," West said, "when I'm a famous designer, we're going to buy a beach house. You'll be able to surf whenever you want."

He already can, I thought. Right now. Right here.

"You both need to eat something," Indira said. "Do you want to get out of those suits first—"

Before she could finish, a shout up the beach interrupted her. We all turned.

"You lying, cheating, thieving son of a—"

I recognized the speaker from around town. His name was Nate Hampton, and he was a used-car salesman and member of Hastings Rock's city council. He was a lanky redhead who had chosen, for some reason known only to God, to wear a suit to the beach. And in that moment, he was charging at another man—the real estate developer, the one West had called Gerry. The redhead crashed into Gerry, and the men went down. They rolled across the sand, throwing wild punches that had neither force nor accuracy. It looked like a couple of pre-teens brawling rather than two grown men.

Deputy Bobby sprinted up the beach, and in a matter of moments, he separated the men. I jogged after him in case he needed help, but since he was Deputy Bobby, he didn't. The redhead was on his knees, wiping a smear of blood at the corner of his mouth. Gerry sat on the sand. He looked older up close, his face lined. Maybe he thought dyeing his goatee and hair made him look younger. In my opinion, it made him look like he'd fallen into the shoe polish.

"Mr. Hampton," Deputy Bobby said to the redhead. "What's going on here?"

"Nothing." The redhead got to his feet. He spat blood on the sand, leveled a furious look at Gerry, and shook his head. Then he took off toward the parking lot.

"Are you all right, sir?" Deputy Bobby asked as he helped Gerry to his feet.

"Fine, fine." But Gerry winced as he pressed a hand to his side.

"Let me get an on-duty deputy over here—"

"No need." Gerry detached himself from Deputy Bobby. People were still staring, and Gerry gave a weak wave. "We're all right here." He patted Deputy Bobby's arm. "Thank you, young man. Now, if you'll excuse me…"

"You should wait for a paramedic to have a look at you. We've got some chairs right over there."

"No, no, no. I'm fine." And with another of those limp waves, Gerry shuffled off toward the cluster of tents that marked the operations center for the surfing challenge.

"I'm going to make sure he's okay," Deputy Bobby said to me.

"Bobby!" West's voice had an unexpected edge as he joined us. "What are you doing?"

Deputy Bobby's face shut down. His gaze settled on something in the middle distance, not quite looking at West.

"The fight—" I began.

"Excuse us," West said to me.

I blinked and opened my mouth, but the only thing I could come up with was "Oh. Yeah. Sorry."

Deputy Bobby was still staring into the middle distance as I retreated.

"We talked about this," West said, his voice sharp and carrying over the crash of the waves. "You're not a deputy anymore. This isn't your responsibility. Your responsibility is your family."

Deputy Bobby said something too low for me to hear.

"What about somebody who's actually on duty?" West said. "Dairek was right there!"

Deputy Bobby spoke again.

When West answered, his voice softened. "What if you'd gotten hurt?"

Then I moved beyond the reach of their voices.

Back at the chairs, the Last Picks were waiting for me with universally miserable expressions. Millie looked like she was about to cry. Keme glared at me as though this were somehow my fault. Indira sighed and started unwrapping a sandwich. And Fox watched Deputy Bobby and West without the slightest attempt to hide their interest.

"That," they said, "is not good."

CHAPTER 2

"But I don't want to go to a party," I said as we bounced along a rutted dirt road in Millie's Mazda3.

"It's going to be fun," Millie said. "In fact, it's going to be AMAZING!"

It had been a long, strange day. We'd gone home and spent the afternoon trying to be normal. Spoiler alert: it didn't work. The fight—fights, I guess, if you count Deputy Bobby and West's spat—had ruined an otherwise perfect day, and nothing seemed capable of dispelling the mood. Maybe that was why, when Millie and Keme and Fox had announced that we were going to a party for the adults who had participated in the surf challenge, I wasn't capable of offering my usual level of resistance.

Now, as we followed the unpaved road under a cloudy night sky, I repeated my point: "But I don't want to go."

"What would you do instead?" Fox asked. "Sit in your room and pretend to write and feel bad about pretending to write?"

"Ouch!"

"I know how it goes, darling. We're not going to let you do that to yourself."

"That sounds like something a cult leader would say right before kidnapping you into their cult."

"My cousin was in a cult!" Millie announced.

"Why am I not surprised?" I murmured.

That made Keme turn around to blast me with a death-ray.

Since I wasn't scared of Keme, like, at all, because I was an adult and I was bigger than him and I was definitely, most certainly stronger, I said, "Also, for everyone's information, I actually was going to write tonight. I was going to write a lot."

Fox cleared their throat.

I sank down in my seat. "Probably."

After that, we finished the drive in silence, with only the rumble of tires and the creak of Millie's suspension as we threaded our way over mile after mile of grassy slopes.

I'd never been in this area before—north of Hastings Rock, on the far side of Klikamuks Head. Even with the cloud cover, the head itself was a bulk of stone and earth protruding into the sea, visible as a patch of deeper darkness across the vista of open ground. Instead of the conifer forests I'd grown accustomed to, tall grasses grew here, and it reminded me more of a Midwestern prairie than, say, the setting for a movie about sexy vampires. The smell of the prairie grass filtered into the car—a dusty, sagey smell that was unexpectedly pleasant.

A chain-link fence stopped us as we approached the surf camp. Signs announced NO TRESPASSING and DO NOT ENTER and DANGER! CONSTRUCTION SITE! Graffiti overlaid many of the signs—THIEVES said one, and another said GET OUT, and another ONE PEOPLE, ONE LAND. Apparently the protesting wasn't only happening at the surf challenge; I wondered if, to some people, this was sacred land too. When Keme stuck his head out of the window, a guy in board shorts and a ratty Hurley hoodie opened the gate for us, and we drove into the camp itself.

"That's some serious security for a surf camp," Fox said.

Millie glanced at Keme before saying, "They've had a lot of problems with vandalism. They put up the fence and the cameras, but it still keeps happening."

Keme nodded.

As we continued into the camp, the gate rolled shut behind us. Ahead, buildings took shape in the darkness: frame structures with clapboard siding and dark shingle roofs. When the headlights washed over them, color popped in the night—doors painted bright reds and blues, shockingly vivid against the monochrome night. In contrast to the pristine new buildings, the surf camp's grounds consisted of churned earth, spilled gravel, and weeds. There was no landscaping, no sidewalks, not even a proper parking lot. Millie ended up parking on a grassy strip where other cars were already clustered.

When we got out of the car, the sound of music came on the night air—I didn't recognize it, but I figured it was probably called something like acoustic surf rock, and it sounded like it would appeal to a group (mostly men) focused on "chillaxin'" and indulging in recreational substances. Behind the camp's central building, firelight flickered and sent the shadows dancing.

We came around the central building and found ourselves in a large, open square. The music was louder here—the voices too. At one end of the square stood a palapa. Under the palm-thatch roof, fairy lights illuminated a fully stocked bar, where several of the surfers were playing mixologist. At the other end of the clearing, a bonfire blazed; the heat lapped at me even from a distance, and a whiff of wood smoke came in on my next breath.

The party appeared to be in full swing, and it seemed to combine elements of beach hangout and Halloween bacchanal. A guy with long blond hair—his costume, apparently, was "lifeguard"—laughed as he staggered and fell, and then he laughed even harder. A girl in a "nurse" bikini—in total defiance of the October cold—was balancing an inflatable ring on her nose while her friends recorded her on their phones. A couple more of the long-haired types (maybe they came in a six pack?) were wrestling—apparently simultaneously trying to turn each other out of their Baja hoodies—and neither of them seemed sober enough to get the upper hand. At the edge of the ring of firelight, someone moved, and I thought I recognized Nate Hampton. After assaulting Gerry at the beach, the redhead had apparently found time to change into a hoodie and jeans, and he didn't look too bothered by the earlier scuffle.

Keme took off into the scrum of bodies (he'd gone with "skeleton in a suit" for his costume, which apparently meant some makeup on his face and a suit that he looked really good in—I was fairly sure Millie had been the intended audience, and I had a sneaking suspicion the suit belonged to Deputy Bobby). Millie went with him. Fox and I lingered at the edge of the square. To their top hat and frock coat, Fox had added a monocle—again, ordinary Fox apparel, or Halloween costume? You decide!

As we stood there, voices came up the path behind us. It only took me a moment to recognize West.

"…because I'm afraid you'll get hurt. Do you understand?"

And Deputy Bobby's answer was quiet and even. "Yes."

"And that's scary for me. That's terrifying, Bobby. Because I love you. And I know we've talked about this before, but that actually makes it worse. You promised me that when you were off duty, you weren't going to do stuff like that. Get involved, I mean. And when you break your promises, it's hard for me to trust you, and trust is the bedrock of our relationship. Do you understand?"

"I understand."

A moment later, they appeared. West was still in his hot-as-the-sun construction worker costume; if anything, he somehow looked even better, but I still had no idea how he wasn't freezing to death. Deputy Bobby was a construction worker too, although, thank God, he'd managed to cover himself up a little more: boots, jeans, a white T-shirt, and then the hi-vis vest and hardhat.

"Pity," Fox murmured. "I was looking forward to seeing your tongue fall out of your mouth."

I shot them a furious look, but by then, West and Deputy Bobby had noticed us.

"Hey," West said in that tone people use when they're trying to pretend everything is great. "I didn't know you guys were coming."

"They made me," I said.

For some reason, that made Deputy Bobby smile—just a quicksilver flash, there and gone.

"Keme and Millie are already out there enjoying themselves," Fox said, jerking a thumb at the crowd. "I've been keeping an eye on the wallflower."

"I hope someone said something to Keme about age-appropriate drinks," Deputy Bobby said.

"Even though that's none of our business tonight," West said. He squeezed Deputy Bobby's hand. "Because we're here as a normal couple, right?"

Deputy Bobby said, "Right."

"Indira talked to him," Fox said. "I don't know what she said, but his eyes were huge when he came out of that kitchen."

"And that's another thing." I turned toward Fox. "Why didn't Indira have to come?"

"Indira didn't have to come because she's an adult and a fully actualized human being."

"I'm an adult. I'm a fully actualized human being."

"Wearing a keyboard cat costume."

"It's not—" I drew a breath through clenched teeth. "You're just saying that because you're scared of her."

"Of course I'm scared of her. My God, Dash, have you seen that woman debone a chicken thigh?"

"Okay, you two have fun," West said. "We're going to get drinks."

Before I realized who he was talking about, he reached out and grabbed my hand and pulled me toward the palapa. I stumbled after him, glanced back, and saw a strange expression on Deputy Bobby's face—like the quicksilver smile, there and then gone, only this hadn't been a smile. Worry, maybe. Or something adjacent to worry.

West led me under the palm-thatch roof of the palapa, and we got in line for the makeshift bar. The crowd around us seemed evenly split between guys who had made a modicum of effort to dress up for Halloween (a cowboy, a police officer, Where's Waldo?), and others who had clearly decided that going as a surfer was costume enough—lots of board shorts, flip-flops, and hoodies. Most of the women, on the other hand, had put a little more work into their getup. I counted two Playboy bunnies, one girl from *Stranger Things*, an evil (but sexy) clown, and no fewer than three Wonder Women. The clink of bottles mixed with the swell of voices, and the music was louder here—more of that acoustic surfer rock. I figured I could stand about ten more minutes of it before I started looking for a power cord to chew on.

"Am I making a mistake?" West asked.

I glanced over at him. His eyes were wet, and he was blinking rapidly, staring straight ahead.

"With Bobby." His voice broke as he added, "Am I screwing everything up?"

"What?" I looked around, but aside from a lot of drunken surfers and one Wonder Woman who was trying to climb on a cowboy's shoulders, there was nobody who could help me. "I don't—"

"I love him so much. But I keep feeling like I'm—like I'm messing up, you know? And you know how Bobby is. It's impossible to read him. He never says what he's thinking. And then I ask him, and he says he loves me, or he's happy, or—I don't know. And I just want to scream." Some of the tears spilled, and as he wiped his cheeks, he ducked his head and said, "Never mind."

I could run away, of course. I could pretend I hadn't heard him. I could simply let the conversation drop—he'd made it possible. I could hope that drunken Wonder Woman fell on me and her armor crushed me to death. (It looked like a possibility; that cowboy was definitely not off-roading material.) But West was still wiping his cheeks and sniffling, and he just looked so…miserable.

"I'm all in favor of screaming," I said and touched his arm. "And crying, for the record. So if you want to do some screaming, we can walk out to the beach, and you can scream your head off. And I'll hold your drink. And then we'll get more drinks. And then I'll hold your hair while you puke. And someone will take pictures of us passed out next to the toilet." The line moved forward, and I said, "I've never actually done this before, so I'm mostly basing this off of movies."

A tiny laugh made his shoulders tremble. He looked up. His eyes were red. (And the really annoying part was that it didn't make him even one percent less gorgeous.)

"Why don't you tell me what's going on?" I asked. "Is this about, uh, the thing at the beach?"

"No." And then he said, "Yes."

"You sound like me."

We both laughed.

"I don't know," West said as we moved forward again. The song changed, but the music didn't. Eight minutes to power cord. "I mean, yes, we argued about that. I argued about it. That's—that's the whole problem. He just agrees with me. And he apologizes. And I know he means it, but—" He was breathing rapidly; the hi-vis vest made it easy to see how his chest and belly rose and fell with shallow breaths. "I don't think he wants to move. And I don't think he's happy. And sometimes—sometimes I think I'm ruining his life. But when I ask him, he says he loves me, and he wants to be with me, and everything's going to be okay."

The couple in front of us stepped aside, and we found ourselves stepping up to the bar. The guy behind it had sleepy eyes, lots of interesting muscles, and a tiny pair of black trunks. It was starting to feel like the *Twilight Zone*. Was I the only person who got cold anymore?

"What's up, kitty cat?" he asked. And then somehow he managed to lean on the bar in a way that made a LOT (cue Millie's voice) of muscles pop in his arms. Like, some of those muscles I hadn't even known existed.

West started giggling.

"Uh," I said.

That made West giggle harder.

"Damian," the guy behind the bar said. He did some more of that very interesting leaning. I was trying to remember how to swallow.

"I'll have a vodka cran," West said through the giggles. "And two beers—an IPA, whatever you've got. What about you, Dash? His name's Dash."

"Hi, Dash," Damian said.

My face was hot. Pins and needles ran across my chest. My throat had closed up.

West was dying by now, but he managed to say, "He'll have a vodka cran too."

As West started to pat himself down (although God only knew where he could be carrying a wallet), the bartender (Damian, said a treacherous voice in my head) shook his head. "Everything's comped. Gerry's picking up the tab."

He must have understood our confusion because he tipped his head toward the clearing. It took me a moment to recognize Gerry in the flickering firelight—the real estate developer had opted not to wear a costume, and he was in deep conversation with a woman dressed as a *luchador*.

"Two vodka crans," Damian said as he set the glasses on the bar. Two bottles of Rock Top's IPA followed. "And two beers."

"Thank you," West sang out. "Say thank you, Dash."

I managed "Thanks."

"See you around, kitty cat."

As we stepped away from the bar, West said in an unnecessarily loud voice, "Oh my God, he is gorgeous! And he's totally your type!"

My face still felt like it was on fire, but the pins-and-needles sensation faded as we left the palapa and moved into the shadows beyond the fairy lights.

"You're welcome, by the way," West said with another giggle. "Now he's definitely going to come find you."

I took a gulp of the vodka cran rather than answer—it was good; not ordinarily my drink, but still good.

Either West took pity on me, or he was still focused on his own problems, because he said, "I don't know what to do. Bobby's the first guy I've ever been in love with. He's the first guy I've ever shared an apartment with. He knows my family; they're obsessed with him, of course. But I feel like we've gone as far as we can in Hastings Rock. Things aren't…progressing. I keep thinking if we don't leave—" He stopped, and his voice had an unexpected catch at the end.

The ideal solution, of course, would be to have a bottomless vodka cran, and to keep drinking until I passed out so that I never had to respond to any of this. But I didn't have a bottomless vodka cran. And West was wiping his eyes again. I drew a deep breath.

"I feel like I need to be totally upfront and tell you I'm terrible at relationships. Like, horrible. So, I don't really feel like I'm qualified to give advice."

"You're my friend," West said. And then he laughed softly. "Besides, who else am I going to ask? Damian?"

"Definitely do not ask Damian. He looks like one thousand percent trouble."

"But hot."

I dodged that one. "I know you said Deputy Bobby isn't very…communicative, I guess." And I didn't say that part of me found that strange, since it always seemed so easy to talk to Deputy Bobby, since it seemed easy to read his expressions—the little furrow between his eyebrows when I'd lost him with an obscure gaming reference, or the way his mouth turned up at the corner when he was trying not to smile, or those times I caught a glimpse of him, and I knew, even though I couldn't have listed the reasons, that he was happy right then, in that moment. That things were good. "But," I continued, "I don't think he's a liar."

"God, no. Bobby is definitely not a liar."

"So, if he's telling you he loves you and that he wants to be with you and that everything will be okay, then that's what he believes."

West sighed, and in a small voice, he said, "I know."

"That's a good thing, right?"

"I don't know. I think it might be what he wants to believe. Or what he thinks he believes. I don't know." West put his hand on his neck, and in a softer voice he said, "I don't know."

"You and Bobby are great together." When I heard what I'd said, a wave of—I don't know what to call it: déjà vu, or disorientation, or maybe just a sense of unreality—swept over me. It was like hearing an echo. That was what everyone had told me. *You and Hugo are great together. You and Hugo are perfect. You and Hugo are such a good match.* And hearing those words come out of my mouth made me feel like I'd stepped off solid ground. I fumbled for words and managed to add, "You're going to figure it out." And then, even though it was like cutting off my own arm, I said, "Maybe you're right. Maybe the move is exactly what you need."

West took a few deep breaths. Then he said, "Thanks, Dash," and kissed my cheek. It ought to have set off all my peopling alarms—CODE RED! CODE RED! PHYSICAL PROXIMITY AND EMOTIONS AND TOUCHING!—but I was surprised that it felt...fine. Sweet, actually. Because West *was* my friend, even if—

I cut off that thought. And then I buried it.

"I guess we should be getting back," West said. Then he giggled again. "Bobby is going to lose his mind when Damian tracks you down."

Before I could ask what that meant—not that I wanted to know, not that I had any interest in why Deputy Bobby might have such a strong reaction to a guy, an admittedly hot guy, a guy with muscles that were like, everywhere (I mean, did *you* know you could have muscles in your back?) who happened to want to, um, talk to me (although I suspected that with Damian, not much talking would be involved)—West started walking, and I hurried to catch up.

When we got back to Deputy Bobby and Fox, Millie and Keme had returned, and the four of them were engaged in conversation with the woman in the *luchador* costume. She carried her mask under one arm, and she looked familiar—she had a long, almost overdeveloped jaw that gave her a distinctive look. Her boyishly short hair was threaded with silver, and she had crow's feet, but otherwise, she looked like she was in her twenties: a hard, muscular body that looked strong from being used in the real world rather than from hours in a gym.

"A beer for you," West said as he handed one of the Rock Tops to Deputy Bobby.

"Thank you," Deputy Bobby said with a small smile, as he slipped an arm around West's waist.

West passed the second bottle to Fox. "And one for you."

"Bless you, my child."

"Sorry, Millie," I said. "I thought you and Keme were still off partying."

"Oh, it's okay," she said. "I don't really like drinking. I'll probably just have a Coke. Sometimes I have just one beer and I feel SO SLEEPY."

The woman in the *luchador* costume rocked slightly on her heels; apparently, she'd never been in Millie's blast zone before.

Gesturing with his beer to the *luchador*, Deputy Bobby said, "Jen was just telling us that Keme's going to do some part-time instruction once the camp is up and running."

Keme was actually, honest-to-God grinning. I gave him a thumbs-up, and his grin immediately changed to a scowl.

"And he'll be full-time once he's eighteen," Jen said. Her voice was deeper than I expected, and for a moment, I wondered if she might be trans. As though she'd heard the thought, she said, "You have no idea how hard it is to find surf instructors who aren't raging homophobes and transphobes."

"Really?" West looked at Deputy Bobby. "You never told me that."

"It's not really an issue here," he said.

Jen shook her head. "It's an issue pretty much everywhere else. Lots of toxic masculinity—they're not too keen on women surfing either, by the way. Lots of machismo. Lots of aggression. And like I said, the homophobia and transphobia are off the charts."

"But this cute guy just tried to pick up Dash," West said. "And Bobby's been surfing for ages."

Deputy Bobby gave me a crooked smile that I couldn't quite read. And then, to my surprise, he reached out and flicked my cat ears.

"Let me guess," Jen said with a mock groan. "Damian?"

West burst out laughing.

"He's a sweetheart," Jen said to me, "and he won't hurt you on purpose. But don't ask him to do long division."

"What do you mean," Deputy Bobby asked—and somehow, his voice matched that crooked smile—"he won't hurt Dash on purpose?"

"Oh God, he's just a mess—can't make up his mind, can't settle down. I hired him because he really is sweet, and like I said, it's hard to find queer surfers, but I bet he'll be gone before we even officially open—he'll go crash with a buddy in Malibu, or he'll be living out of a van on Oahu. He's good with cars, so he'll pick up some easy money and move on again. Sorry; I'm telling you so he doesn't break your heart."

Deputy Bobby made a weird, sharp noise. West turned to look at him. Fox raised an eyebrow. Millie's eyes got huge. And Keme, of course, glared at me like somehow I was ruining everything. It took me a moment to realize the noise had been a laugh.

Into the silence, I said, "So, this is going to be a surf camp for LGBTQ people?"

"It's a surf camp for everyone," Jen said. "But with a zero-tolerance policy for that kind of BS. It's an untapped market, see? There are a lot of queer people who either want to surf or are surfing, but they don't have a community. On top of that, you've got a perfect situation here—ideal conditions for cold-water surfing, plus Portland's already got a strong LGBTQ population, and it doesn't hurt that it's one of the most beautiful places in the world." Then she gave Deputy Bobby a pointed look. "That's if I can get the right instructors."

With a laugh, Deputy Bobby said, "I'd like to—"

"We're moving," West said. "So, he can't."

The bonfire snapped and popped.

"As I was saying," Jen began, "maybe a few weekends every month."

"Maybe," West said. "I don't know. We're going to be really busy."

The expression on Deputy Bobby's face might have been the flickering light of the fire, but I didn't think so.

"Keme won't be too busy," Millie said. "And Keme's SO good with kids. He'd love to do it. Right, Keme? He can start whenever you want. He can start TONIGHT!"

"We're not quite ready to start," Jen said. "But we should be good to go by the spring."

"It's going to be a huge success," Deputy Bobby said. "I know you weren't actually competing, but I saw you out there today; anybody who comes here is going to be lucky to have you as a teacher."

Jen laughed. "I don't know about that, but it's kind of you to say. It gets harder every year. That's the whole reason I needed to make this camp happen now—I'm calling it my retirement in my thirties. Come on, I'll introduce you to some of the other guys."

She led Fox, Deputy Bobby, West, Keme, and Millie toward the crowd gathered around the bonfire. I hung back. Deputy Bobby must have noticed, because he turned to check where I was; I gave him a wave to let him know I was fine.

Fine, yes, but I needed a few minutes to myself. In part, it was because of all those people. The thought of smiling and nodding and trying to remember names and the need to say something clever or funny or cute, all of it getting sharper and sharper by the moment—no, thank you. Plus, everything with West had left me unmoored. So, I stayed at the edge of the square, my hand aching with the cold of the vodka cran, and watched.

I'd always been good at watching. Grist for the mill, you know? One day, I might write a story about Will Gower where he was nursing his drink (definitely not a vodka cran—probably a whiskey highball, although maybe we'd go back to gimlets) and watching a man across a darkened clearing. That man would have golden skin and broad shoulders and hair so dark it looked like each perfect strand had been inked into place. He'd have remarkable bronze eyes that widened when he had no idea what you were saying, but you could tell he still found it amusing. Found you amusing. And he'd be leaving. Going away forever. Maybe the mob, I thought. Maybe he'd gotten in trouble somehow. In a mystery story, you needed external problems as well as internal ones.

A footstep scuffed the ground, and I turned. The man seemed to take shape as he got closer: white, middle-aged, stocky build, hair and goatee the color of coal dust. Gerry, the real estate developer. Something about his walk looked a little...lubricated, if you know what I mean, and when he got closer, the smell of booze and sweat and wood smoke mingled.

"Gerry Webb," he said and stuck out his hand. I shook. He had rough, dry skin—not calluses, but like he might need a good exfoliator/moisturizer combo.

"Dash Dane."

"I know. I've had my eye on you."

He held on to my hand a beat too long. Maybe his grin was supposed to be friendly, but I'd had other guys give me that grin before. Damian the bartender, if he were thirty years older, would have given me a grin like that.

"Nice to meet you." And then inspiration struck, and I held up my drink. "Thanks for the drink. And for sponsoring the surfing competition."

"Cost of doing business, cost of doing business. You want something to be a success, you've got to get people talking."

"Is the surf camp one of your projects too?"

"Darn tootin'." He patted himself down as though searching for something, and then he gave up. "You're a very nice-looking young man, you know."

"Uh. Thank you." I scrambled for the right thing to say next and came up with "How do you know Jen?"

Gerry eyed me, wobbling under the influence of his drinks. I could feel the challenge—or the demand, or the insistence, whatever you wanted to call it— building. But then his face relaxed. "Don't know her. We were both trying to get the city council to approve developments. She thought I was going to ruin her little camp. I showed her how helpful it can be to have somebody on your side—somebody who knows how to get things done. Somebody who's got the money to make things happen."

"And she brought you on as an investor?"

"Oh sure. She knew she wasn't going to get anywhere with her camp, not without some help. She needed a guy with some experience. A guy who knows how to take care of the people he cares about." Another of those drunken wobbles. The firelight danced in his glassy eyes. He put a hand on my arm, and I tried to convince myself he was just trying to keep his balance. Then his thumb stroked lightly over my biceps. "That's the advantage to having a mature partner," he said, his voice gravelly with the drink and, maybe, something else. "I know how to take care of someone."

I turned, doing my best to keep the movement casual, to glance at where Deputy Bobby and the others had joined the crowd around the bonfire. A long-haired surfer was trying to walk on his hands, while another surfer guy threw pebbles at him and tried to get him to fall. Everybody was watching. Everybody was laughing. Even if I shouted—the thought came dizzily up from somewhere inside me—even if I shouted, I wasn't sure they'd realize it wasn't just one more person shouting in the crowd.

The movement was enough to make Gerry drop his hand, but when I turned back to face him, he was watching me even more intently. "I wanted to talk to you, you know," he said. "I told you I've had my eye on you."

"I'm sorry," I said, "but I just got out of a relationship—"

His laugh boomed out into the night. For a moment, he didn't seem to be as drunk as I'd thought. There was something knowing in his face—a hard, sharp knowing that I didn't like. "I wanted to talk to you," he said, exaggerated amusement lacing the words, "about that sweet little piece you're sitting on." My mind could only conjure one horrifying interpretation of those words, which must have been obvious because Gerry laughed and said, "The land. That old house too, I suppose, but the land."

"Oh."

He laughed some more.

"Right," I said. "The land. Well, see, I'm not sure Hemlock House really is mine. It's a strange situation—"

"I know all about strange situations. I've got lawyers who love a strange situation. And I could make you a good offer. Girasol II – the second phase of development. I've already sold every lot of Girasol I. And you could use the money. It's got to be tough, being a creative type. Creative types are like Jen, you know. They need a partner. They need someone to take care of them."

His gaze was full of that demand again, and I remembered how his hand had felt clutching mine, and how it had felt when he'd caught my arm. I pulled my eyes away. I found myself looking over his shoulder, past him, at the palapa. Damian was still behind the bar, and he was staring back at us, his jaw set, his mouth a flat line.

"When I come to a new town," Gerry said as he stepped closer, "I like to get to know the people there. Become part of the community. See, that's how I know all about you. And you're a little peach of a kid, easy on the eyes." He touched my stomach, pawing at me through my shirt. "Just lovely."

I took a step back. The paralyzing anxiety that had held me in place shattered, and I said, "Don't touch me."

"Hey," Gerry said and grabbed my arm. "Don't be like that."

I started to pull away. Distantly, I was aware of the vodka cran slipping from my hand.

Gerry's fingers tightened.

And then Deputy Bobby was there, shooting out of the darkness. He got between me and Gerry, planted both hands on Gerry's chest, and shoved. Gerry stumbled back, arms windmilling. Somehow, he stayed upright and caught his balance. His mouth twisted into a snarl, and he said, "You're going to regret that—"

Before he could finish, Deputy Bobby punched him.

Gerry dropped. It wasn't a fall or a stagger. It was like someone had cut a puppet's strings.

Deputy Bobby loomed over him, breathing hard, shaking out a fist. "He said don't touch him!"

West's voice came out of the darkness: "Bobby! Bobby, what are you—"

But Deputy Bobby was still focused on Gerry, and he shouted again, "He told you not to touch him!"

Out of the flickering shadows, West materialized. He stumbled to a stop, staring first at Gerry, then at Deputy Bobby. He grabbed Deputy Bobby's arm.

Deputy Bobby's move was reflexive: an automatic yank to get free of West's hold.

West held on, though, and snapped, "Bobby!"

Deputy Bobby raised his head like someone waking up. He looked at West and blinked as though he didn't recognize him. His gaze came to me, and I didn't know the Deputy Bobby on the other side of the burnished bronze.

"Come on," West said. And then, more harshly, "Come on!"

He towed Deputy Bobby into the darkness.

"Why don't we step away?" Fox asked.

I startled at the sound of their voice; I hadn't realized anyone else was there, but now it seemed like someone had fast-forwarded a movie: Jen was helping Gerry to his feet, and Keme was standing in front of Millie like he intended to be the last line of defense, and more of the surfers and their friends were drifting into a ring to stare at us. With a wild shout, Gerry ripped free from Jen's support and stumbled away from the growing crowd.

Fox laid a hand on my back to get me moving. We started around the camp's central building, heading back to Millie's car, and excited voices exploded into conversation behind us. I tried not to hear the words, and I focused instead on taking slow, deep breaths. As we moved into the darkness, the night air was cold and sweet, free of wood smoke and cannabis vapor and tasting faintly like dew and dune grass and the vodka cran on my breath.

"Well," Fox said, "that was certainly something—"

"I already told you why!" West's voice sliced through the night. It came from somewhere nearby—behind one of the camp buildings. "I don't know why we have to keep having this conversation."

"That was battery," Deputy Bobby said. I'd never heard his voice like that, I thought. Like stamped steel.

"And you're off duty. I want one night, Bobby. One. One night when I get to have a boyfriend who cares about me, who wants to be with me, who is focused on me."

"That's not fair."

"You want to know what's not fair? What's not fair is that every time we go out, you're a deputy, and I'm—I'm an afterthought. I'm whatever you're doing when you aren't breaking up fights or driving drunks home or—" West's voice rose. "Or getting in fights like you're a stupid teenager!"

The night had a heartbeat. My face was hot. Fox sucked in slow, pained breaths.

Deputy Bobby's voice was strained when he said, "I think we should have this conversation after we both cool down."

West expressed his feelings about that idea. At length. With words.

When he finished, Deputy Bobby's familiar tread moved away into the night.

"God," Fox said, and that seemed to break the spell. They got me moving again. "Poor kids."

When we got to Millie's Mazda, Fox tried the doors, but they were locked. "Stay here," they said. "I'm going to get Millie and Keme, and we'll head back to town."

"No, don't. I shouldn't have—they were so excited about this party. I ruined it."

"You didn't ruin it. A lecherous old man ruined it."

"God, West sounded so mad."

In the dark, it was impossible to make out Fox's face, but their voice was strangely uncertain when they said, "Dash—" And then they stopped. In a different voice, they said, "It'll be fine. They'll be fine."

I didn't say anything. It was the first time, as far as I could tell, that Fox had lied to me.

"Wait here," Fox said. "I'll be right back."

Their steps moved off, and the dark bulk of their body dissolved into the night.

I replayed the conversation between Deputy Bobby and West. And then I replayed it again. And then again. I heard in my head, over and over, Deputy Bobby's heavy steps as he walked off. I went over every instant of my interaction with Gerry. I came up with a dozen things I should have done differently. I should have left. As soon as I caught that weird vibe, I should have left. The first time he touched my arm, I should have left. I should have slapped him. I should have said, *If you touch me again, I'm going to call the police.* I should have done anything except stand there, petrified by the thought of making a terrible situation even worse by drawing attention to myself.

And because of me, Deputy Bobby was out there, alone—hurt and angry and confused.

Before I could think about what I was doing, I pushed off from Millie's car. I headed in the direction I had heard Deputy Bobby's steps moving. Off in the distance, the party sounded like it had returned to normal. A man jeered. A woman screamed with delight. A splash, and then a swell of laughter. My vision was slowly adjusting to the night, and the outlines of the buildings solidified, with tunnels of darkness between them. I followed one of those tunnels, passing clapboard cabins that would stand empty until spring, my steps echoing back from painted doors, the smell of freshly sawed wood hanging in the air.

The cabins stopped, and I climbed a low hill, following a footpath beaten into the dirt through the dune grass. The grass whispered against me, scratching the backs of my hands. On the other side of the dune, the beach opened up. A few jagged tears in the clouds gave enough light for me to make out the arc of sand and, beyond it, the restless shimmer of the water. Against a board-and-batten lifeguard tower, surfboards were racked and ready for the next day. Wetsuits hung on wooden drying racks. A striped beach ball, slightly deflated, nestled in the sand.

Movement to the north caught my eye. The ground there rose steeply into bluffs, and the face of the stone caught the night's light so that it had a soft, salt-lamp glow. Against the gentle radiance of the stone, a figure was making its way along the beach.

"Deputy Bobby!"

The crash of the waves swallowed my voice. I wasn't sure the figure—if it even was Deputy Bobby—heard me; if they did, they didn't look back. But I thought I recognized the way they moved, the cut-out shape of them against the pale stone.

I started after them. The sand gave under every step, slowing me. The sound of the breakers grew as I angled past the wrack line, stepping over tangles of kelp and seagrass and a crusty Fanta bottle (empty, of course). The smell of decay met me, and then the wind whipped it away again.

And then I lost them. The figure, whoever it was I'd been following, was gone. I strained, trying to make out movement in the darkness. Nothing.

"Deputy Bobby!"

My words were lost to the winds and the waves.

Pulling out my phone, I trudged in the direction I'd last seen him. I turned on the phone's flashlight. It made it easier to see where I was putting my feet, but it ruined my night vision. I turned the flashlight off again, and then I couldn't see anything. Somehow, the ocean sounded even louder. Maybe the tide was coming in. Was this the right time? I had no idea. I picked up the pace. It was easier going now as I followed the narrow strip of beach along the face of the cliffs. Waves slapped down hard to my left, and the swash rolled up, missing my sneakers by inches. This had been a bad idea, I decided. Deputy Bobby—if it even was Deputy Bobby—wanted to be left alone. That's the whole reason he'd walked away. He was upset, and he needed some time to calm down, to get control of himself. He wouldn't appreciate me barging in on him, even if I was doing it out of friendship.

And then, ahead of me, against the pale luminescence of the stone, I made out a shape. The swash came in again, swirling around that dark bulk. It took me a moment to realize it wasn't a rock. It was someone lying on the ground.

"Bobby?" I started to run. "Bobby!"

But when I reached him, it wasn't Deputy Bobby. It was Gerry Webb, and he was dead.

It looked like he'd fallen—his body shattered by the impact. I couldn't help myself; I looked up. And there, on the cliff above me, someone was looking down. They were too far away for me to make out more than their shape. But they were there.

And then they were gone.

CHAPTER 3

Deputies came. They hauled lights out to the beach, portable generators, protective barriers—to preserve the crime scene, I knew. It was a losing battle; nothing could keep back the tide. I stood there and waited. In the glare of the LEDs, with the waves crashing louder and louder, men and women calling back and forth to each other, it felt like I'd stepped out of my body and into a movie.

Deputy Salkanovic, who went by Salk and had been Hastings Rock's star quarterback (take that however you want), and who got compliments from little old ladies when he wrote them speeding tickets, and who had once—when I'd stopped by the station for some reason—shouted, *Dash-y, my man!* and then given me double high fives—walked me back to the surf camp, and he let me sit in his cruiser with the heater running. A little later, Deputy Dahlberg—who had moved here to learn how to paint and who now gave a weekly class called "Rip His Head Off: Self-Defense through Video Games," who still wore her hair in a blond Rachel cut, and who had once spent fifteen minutes telling me who in the sheriff's office had, um, carnal knowledge of whom (Deputy Bobby earned some extra points that day for, apparently, being smart enough not to play on his own doorstep)—brought me some coffee from a thermos.

I asked Salk about Deputy Bobby. I asked Dahlberg.

Nobody knew where he was.

And then Sheriff Acosta opened the door of the cruiser, leaned down, and said, "Hello, Mr. Dane."

Sheriff Acosta was stocky, with warm brown skin and her hair in a ponytail. I wasn't sure I'd ever seen her not in uniform, and her only affectation—if it was one—was to gel her baby hairs to her forehead, where they almost hid a neat little scar. Although Acosta hadn't been sheriff when I'd been framed for Vivienne Carver's death, she still seemed to hold it against me that I hadn't happily gone along with my own conviction. She'd been even less happy when, a few months later, I'd helped my ex, Hugo, prove his innocence.

I told her everything—not that there was much to tell: how Gerry had assaulted me; how Deputy Bobby had stepped in; the argument with West; and then my decision, if you could call it that, to check on Deputy Bobby and make sure he was okay. I told her about the figure I'd seen moving against the backdrop of the bluffs, and then finding Gerry's body, and then the figure I'd seen above me on the cliffs, looking down at me.

When I finished, the sheriff said, "That's a long way from camp. Why'd you need to talk to him so bad?"

"I just told you." Acosta didn't reply, so I said, "He was upset."

Acosta still didn't say anything. In her silence, I heard a bigger, larger silence—the party was over, a distant part of my brain noted. And I thought I heard a question.

"I understand," Acosta finally said, "there was an altercation."

"What?"

"You mentioned that Deputy Mai stepped in when Mr. Webb put his hands on you. But according to several witnesses, it was more than that: Deputy Mai punched Mr. Webb hard enough to knock Mr. Webb to the ground. Then Deputy Mai stood over Mr. Webb, threatening him."

"That's not—" I almost said *true*. Because it wasn't true, the way she was saying it. Deputy Bobby hadn't—I mean, yes, technically, he had. But it hadn't felt like that. It hadn't been like that. "—the way it was. He did punch Gerry, yes. But only to get him away from me. And Gerry only fell because he'd had too much to drink."

"Was Deputy Mai intoxicated?"

That big silence rushed in again.

"Hold on," I said. "You think Deputy Bobby had something to do with this? That's ridiculous."

"All I'm asking is if Deputy Mai had been drinking."

"He had a beer. One. He wasn't drunk. He certainly wasn't out of control or aggressive or—I can't believe this!"

"Is there anything else you want to tell me?"

"I told you about the person I saw on the cliffs. Why aren't you out there looking for them?"

Acosta's face didn't change as she straightened. She rapped on the hood of the cruiser. "Think about it, Mr. Dane. Believe it or not, the best thing you can do for everyone involved is tell me everything."

"I *am* telling you everything—hey!"

But Sheriff Acosta didn't look back.

A moment later, Salk ducked down to look into the back seat. "Sheriff told me to drive you home. Your friends already left."

"You don't actually believe Bobby had something to do with this."

Salk gave me an embarrassed half-smile, his cheeks flooding with color. "Dash," he said with a weird little shrug. "Come on."

He drove me back to Hemlock House.

I called Deputy Bobby; he didn't answer.

I did not sleep.

Okay, I did. But it was awful; I slipped back and forth between sleeping and waking, hanging on the gray edge of dreams. I dreamed that I was following Deputy Bobby, only then it wasn't Deputy Bobby, and then he was following me, and he was Gerry Webb with the side of his head cracked open, and he had his hands on me.

I was up at the crack of dawn: eight-thirty. My body ached. My head throbbed. Even with the house warm and snug against the October cold, it was hard to drag myself out of bed. I showered. I dressed—my usual getup, which meant a gamer tee (it said CLASSICALLY TRAINED and showed an Atari controller), my canvas jacket, jeans (which Deputy Bobby had once called hipster drainpipes, and Keme had laughed so hard that soda had come out of his nose), and my Mexico 66s (white).

I made my way down to the kitchen. Today, more than usual, the house had a vast, echoing quality, like every sound I made was magnified. Part of me knew that it was only because the house was empty; when Indira and Keme and Fox and, especially, Millie were here, the house felt alive. And part of me knew it was also because I had found Gerry Webb after he died, and I was still processing everything from the night before. In that regard, Hemlock House was probably the perfect place to be—ideal conditions for brooding about mortality and death and dying and the inevitability of dying. If you love damask wallpaper, pocket doors, weird Victorian taxidermy under glass cloches (one was of a tabby cat playing croquet, I kid you not), and a constant reminder that all things must pass and that we, too, are dust returning to dust—well, have I got a place for you.

When I got to the kitchen, the only sound came from the refrigerator's motor. I did not spy a single treat, cake, cookie, crumble, Danish, or other unspecified breakfast pastry. Which was, of course, totally fair. Indira wasn't my servant or my employee. She was my friend, and she loved cooking and baking, and I, of course, happened to benefit from that. But I also wasn't sure I was brave enough to risk making something for myself. A few weeks before, I'd finally worked up the gumption to break out the toaster. Indira hadn't gotten mad—well, she hadn't raised her voice at least. But we'd had a long—LONG, as Millie would put it—conversation about, among other things, toast sweat.

I still hadn't heard anything from Deputy Bobby, so I tried his phone again. It rang until it went to voicemail. I debated leaving a message, disconnected, and sent him a text instead: *Are you okay?* Very smooth, if I do say so myself.

I grabbed my keys, got the Jeep out of the coach house, and headed into town. It's not a far drive; Hemlock House is still technically within the city limits, even though it feels like we're out in the middle of nowhere. That's because of the old-growth forest between Hemlock House and Hastings Rock proper: spruce and pine and cedar, their branches strung with fog and moss, ferns bristling at the side of the road. Today, the fog was the exact color of the sky. Yesterday's perfect weather had disappeared under the blanket of clouds that had moved in overnight, and the light had a thin, streaked quality that made it impossible to tell the time. (The clock said nine, and honest to God, how did people get up this early every day?)

When I'd first moved to Hastings Rock, I'd believed (thank you, phone) that Chipper was the town's only coffee shop. That wasn't technically true—coffee was part of the culture in the Pacific Northwest, and even a town as small as Hastings Rock had multiple options. But Chipper was the only coffee shop in a normal building. The others were drive-thru coffee stands, little frame structures the size of a garden shed, and they were all over the place—in the Box Bros lumber yard's parking lot, next to the Shell service station, on the side of the road just before Bay Bridge.

And because Chipper was the only coffee shop where people could, you know, go inside, it got the bulk of the tourist traffic, and a large share of the locals as well. It didn't hurt that it had a prime location: on Main Street, a couple of blocks from the water, with a great view of Hastings Rock's adorable downtown: a hodgepodge of Victorian and modern coastal and even a few Cape Cods (one was a toothache-inducing pastel pink).

Chipper lived up to its name. The building was painted bright yellow, inside and out, and patrons were invited to draw on the walls—the unofficial theme was smiley faces and/or shining suns. Pretty much every inch of available space was covered, but that didn't stop people from trying. Today, for example, JaDonna, who occasionally did clerical work for the county and whose husband worked at the timber yard and who had what I thought of as church hair, was helping a little boy trace a circle on the wall (presumably, the beginning of either a sun or a face). Driftwood accents made the space feel cozy, and the booths and seating clusters were all occupied, even though tourist season was over. Cyd Wofford was holding his morning Marx study (like a Bible study, but, you know) with Brad Newsum (Newsum Decorative Rock) and Princess McAdams (who was not, disappointingly, a real princess, but who did always carry a loaded shotgun in the rack of her old Ram). Aric Akhtar was reading on his iPad (*The Oregonian* first, then the *Los Angeles Times*, and then *Us Weekly*). Somehow, he was impervious to the clamor. The sealed concrete floor and the large open area meant that Chipper was noisy—the screech of the espresso machine, the overlapping voices, some sort of soft pop that made me think my inner teenage Dash would have loved to come here to wear a beanie and read poetry. The air smelled like good coffee and warm carbs and just a hint of the sea.

"DASH!"

Did I mention the acoustics?

Behind the counter, Millie was jumping up and down. Waving. With both hands. And then, in case I missed her, she cupped her hands around her mouth and—

"DASH! OVER HERE!"

Every eye turned toward me. I was so busy trying to crawl inside my own jacket that it took a moment to register Keme, who was sitting on a stool that he'd pulled over to the service counter. (Tessa, the owner, wouldn't allow him to hang out with Millie in the employees-only area.) Keme looked like he was enjoying my latest round of social panicking; he found a lot of pleasure in the little things.

"Hi, Millie," I said, and I even offered a tiny wave—which only made me blush harder—as I worked my way over to the counter.

Tessa offered a sympathetic smile. She looked tired, but then, she usually did—it might have been a homeostatic response to Millie's constant caffeinated buzz. "Morning, Dash. What can I get you?"

"As a famous artist once said, 'Life is meaningless, and I've wasted the precious seconds I've been given, and we're all just sand running through the hourglass of fate, please pass the bacon.'"

"Fox was having a day, huh?"

"Honestly, I don't even know if it was a bad day, but they certainly ate a lot of bacon."

"Bacon, egg, and cheese on Asiago?"

"Yep."

She started to key it in.

"Actually," I said.

Because Keme is a traitor, he groaned.

"I was thinking about some sausage."

I couldn't hear him, but I knew Keme must have said something because Millie burst into uncontrollable giggles.

"Never mind," I said, "I'll have the farmhouse."

"Not the bacon, egg, and cheese," Tessa said. "Or the sausage."

"That's right. The awesome avocado."

"It's not his fault," Millie said in answer to more of Keme's groans.

Tessa must have taken pity on me because she smiled and said, "Tell you what: I'm going to make you the Dash special. How does that sound?"

"Terrifying. And probably like it stays up too late. And it needs to spend more time brushing its teeth."

She laughed, but apparently she took that as a yes because she asked, "And what about something to drink?"

Keme groaned again. Dramatically.

"The caramel apple latte did look good," I said, "but, on the other hand, there's a case to be made for the salted caramel mocha, and—"

"I'll bring you something you'll like."

"Does it come in Big Gulp size?"

She laughed, and she took my money, and she shooed me away. Which is to say, Tessa knows how to run a good coffee shop.

I dragged a stool over to the counter, ignoring Keme's death glare. Millie came around to hug me—I swear I heard my ribs creak—and then she said, "Dash, are you okay? We were so WORRIED! Keme ALMOST CRIED!"

Keme's eyes got huge, and he shook his head frantically.

"That's so sweet," I said.

He tried to kick me, but I dodged.

"I knew you were a softy."

He tried again, but this time, Millie got in the way. She rubbed my arm and looked into my eyes, and I thought I was about five seconds away from getting another of those rib-pulverizing hugs. "That must have been terrible last night. How are you doing?"

"All right, I guess." She was still looking at me, and for all her volume and energy and general excitability, Millie had a way of looking at you so that you knew she was seeing you, and that she cared, and that if she ruptured your eardrums, it was only because she loved you. I felt myself sink down onto the stool, and I propped an elbow on the counter. "I mean, it's weird. I didn't like him, obviously. He was a creep. And I would have been happy never to see him again. But I didn't want anything bad to happen to him, and when I found him—"

"You felt guilty," Millie said softly.

"I guess so. Because I was so mad at him. And I did want something bad to happen to him, maybe. Just not that." I shook my head. "I don't know. It was a terrible night."

Millie rubbed my arm some more. "And you didn't even get the number of that cute bartender."

"Well, that wasn't really—"

"And Bobby had to FIGHT someone for you."

I tried to give her a look. "Yeah, like I said, it was terrible—"

"And then Bobby and WEST got in a fight because Bobby had to save you." When I didn't say anything, she asked, "Remember?"

Keme was biting the collar of his ancient Quiksilver tee, trying not to laugh.

"Yes, Millie. I remember. Like I said: it was terrible."

Maybe it was my tone. Millie's face fell, and she rubbed my arm some more. Keme, for his part, finally managed to kick me in the leg, but it was gentle, and the look on his face was concerned, so I decided to consider it a love tap.

"Here we go," Tessa announced as she joined us. She passed a tray to me. "The Dash Special."

It had four quarters of bagel arranged neatly on the plate. Not one bagel cut into four pieces; four different bagels—Asiago, everything, plain, and whole wheat. And the sandwiches themselves looked different. I spied ham on one. Sausage on another. Avocado, definitely. And, gods be praised, bacon.

"Campfire s'mores latte," she added as she handed me an enormous mug. "Not quite a Big Gulp; there are probably legal considerations if we make them any bigger."

"You're the single greatest human who's ever lived."

Tessa laughed.

"You're a saint crossed with an angel crossed with a taco."

Keme rolled his eyes. But that didn't stop him from taking the ham and egg bagel quarter from my plate.

"Millie," Tessa said, "I need you to restock."

"Oh, right. Sure." But Millie's eyes cut to me. "I'll do it right now, Tessa."

Tessa sighed. "In five minutes."

"Thank you, Tessa!"

Already walking away, Tessa gave a lazy wave over her shoulder with a bar towel.

I tried to eat, but I didn't have much of an appetite. Fortunately, Keme was more than willing to help—for such a short, skinny kid, he knew how to pack it away. I focused on my latte, which was chocolatey and marshmallowy and, yes, coffee-y, and all around amazing. My headache shrank to a manageable size. And although I still wished I could have slept to a reasonable hour, I did feel a little better.

"Have you talked to Bobby?" Millie asked.

I shook my head. "You?"

Keme grimaced. Millie said, "We haven't seen him since, you know, the fight. We waited for you, and then the deputies told us to go home, and—" Her voice thinned. "He's okay, right?"

"I'm sure he's fine," I said. "I think he's got bigger things to worry about than an argument with West, though. The way Sheriff Acosta was asking questions, it sounds like they're looking at him for Gerry's murder."

Keme frowned around a mouthful of my bacon, egg, and cheese bagel. Millie glanced over at him.

"What?" I asked.

"What makes you think that?"

"I told you: Acosta kept asking about Bobby, about that stupid fight." I was so upset that I forgot I wasn't hungry and polished off the rest of the farmhouse bagel sandwich. "It wasn't even a fight. I mean, Bobby punched him. Once. That's all."

"No, I mean, what made you think it's a murder?"

"Because someone pushed Gerry off that cliff. I saw them."

Millie looked at Keme.

Keme snatched the final quarter of bagel and took a savage bite.

"Will you just tell me already?" I said.

"Well, everyone thinks Gerry fell."

Coffeehouse pop played softly in the background. Chairs scraped across the sealed concrete flooring. A grown man (we're talking late forties) was whining to his mom that his frappe had too much whipped cream.

"That's ridiculous," I said. "I told the sheriff I saw someone. I saw someone on the beach last night, and I saw someone on the cliff."

"Right," Millie said. "Totally. And we believe you."

Keme grunted around a mouthful of avocado, egg, and cheese to suggest that he might not believe me.

"It's just…" Millie shrugged.

"Who told you it wasn't a murder?"

"Dairek."

"Dairek?" I barely managed not to say that Deputy Dairek flirted with every female tourist under the age of fifty, had an uncanny ability to find a way to bring up the fact that he was a deputy, still lived with his mom, and had once gotten caught in his own zipper in the restroom of the Otter Slide. (I'd been there. I'd heard the screams.) Instead, I managed to say, "Dairek doesn't get to decide the manner of death. That's up to the district medical examiner. And there's no way the district medical examiner has already made a decision; in the first place, it's been less than twenty-four hours, and in the second, it's a weekend." I tried to stop, but I kept going. "And I might not be a cop, but I've done enough research to know that with any suspicious death, the appropriate course of action is to treat it as if it were a homicide. That way you don't lose valuable evidence. This is a procedural travesty."

"Uh, right," Millie said, "but I think they did investigate, and they didn't find anything."

"But I didn't want *any* whipped cream," the fortysomething wailed behind us. "And now it *touched* it!"

"That's impossible," I said. I was so outraged that I barely noticed Keme had stolen my s'mores latte and was now guzzling it. "That's ridiculous. I saw somebody on the cliff! I'm an eyewitness!"

Which, okay, might have been stretching it a tiny bit.

Keme gave Millie a significant look over the rim of the mug, and her cheeks colored.

"There's more?" I asked.

"Uh, no."

Keme was still looking at her.

"What?" I asked. "What aren't you telling me?"

"It's nothing, really. I mean, it was just Dairek, you know. I don't think it's what the sheriff or—"

"Millie," I said.

The words left her in a rush: "Dairek says you're making it up for attention."

I said some words that you can't say around your grandma.

The fortysomething dropped his frappe, and his mom (who had to be in her sixties) covered his ears and led him out of Chipper.

A little girl who had been drawing smiley faces on the wall repeated one of the, uh, words. Loudly.

Keme's eyes got huge, and the corner of his mouth started to twitch.

"Sorry," I mumbled. I mumbled it a few times, in various directions, making sure Aric and Cyd and Brad all heard me apologize. I said sorry again to Tessa, who waved it off with a pained smile. I said sorry to the mom of the little girl (like Keme, the mom looked like she was trying not to laugh).

"Dash—" Millie said.

"Thanks for letting me know," I said.

I slipped off my stool and headed for the door.

But when I got to the Jeep, I sat there, hands wrapped around the steering wheel.

I had not imagined someone on the cliffs. My eyes had not been tricking me. I was not an Edwardian heroine prone to hysterics. (I probably would have been, though, if I'd been alive then.) I knew what I'd seen.

I shifted into drive and drove north out of town.

CHAPTER 4

By day, the surf camp looked different. The gate was open, for one thing. The graffiti was more prominent. In the thin, tintype light, weeds poked through mounds of displaced earth. The clapboard buildings had a rough, unfinished look that the darkness had concealed. Flattened cans and plastic bottles lay tangled in scrubby clumps of grass. When I got out of the Jeep, the smell of marijuana met me.

I made my way to the central building, but it was locked and dark. Then I walked around it toward the square where, the night before, they'd had their party. The wind made a high-pitched noise as it whipped down the corridor of cabins, and the blued steel of the clouds rolled steadily overhead. The light was so diffuse that there were no real shadows, and it made the world feel disconnected from reality, outside of space and time.

The surf camp's central square was in shambles. The bonfire had burned itself down to ash and the charred ends of logs. More trash—bottles, cups, vape pods, paper napkins, a forgotten shoe—stretched from the bonfire all the way to the palapa. A camp chair lay on its side. A drying puddle of vomit marked where someone had failed to make it to the restroom. Someone had tied an empty garbage bag to one of the palapa's supports, and now it flapped like a black wing every time the wind picked up. There was no laughter, no friendly voices, no surf rock. A hint of old smoke made the air greasy.

I was still standing there, trying to decide what I wanted to do, when a guy emerged from the restrooms. He had dark hair under a beanie, and he wore a Baja hoodie and what appeared to be hemp pants with, yes, flip-flops. He picked a path over to the palapa and, apparently unconcerned that it was still morning, began mixing himself a drink at the bar. He put most of it back on his first try, and he finished on his second. He was setting down the glass when he noticed me and said, "Oh shoot."

(He didn't say shoot.)

Damian looked, well, rough this morning. His voice was rough too, like he hadn't spoken yet today, and even from across the square, I could see he had dark hollows under his eyes. His color wasn't great, and he didn't seem too steady on his feet.

"Hey," he said and began making his way toward me. He tried for a smile and got three-quarters of the way there. "Dan, right? I tried to catch up with you last night."

"Dash."

His expression veered toward sheepish. "Almost."

I laughed in spite of myself. I have a weak spot for men who are human disasters, mostly because I'm one myself. "I'm surprised you remember any of it. Looks like you had quite the night."

"Oh my God," he groaned, and rubbed his eyes. I caught a whiff of rum, sweet on his breath. "Kids these days. I'm telling you, they have no respect for their elders. A bunch of eighteen-year-olds lining up shots and telling me I'm an old man if I can't keep up."

I took a closer look at him. He'd been clean shaven the night before, but now he had a hint of stubble, and I was surprised to see gray in it. "Old man, huh? Let me guess: you've reached the venerable age of twenty-five."

"Thirty." That sheepish grin again. "I tell them twenty-eight."

"Bull plop."

(I did not say bull plop.)

That made him laugh.

"I'm almost thirty," I said. "Nobody who's thirty has abs like you do."

"Hard work, my guy." The smile definitely wasn't sheepish now, and I couldn't quite bring myself to meet the look in his eyes. "And good genes."

The wind shrieked down the path at us. Damian shivered. The empty garbage bag flapped madly.

"Hey," he said. "I'm really glad you came back. I've got a couple of those little gremlins in my cabin, but what do you say we grab some bottles, and we'll find somewhere quiet to...chill?"

It was simultaneously sweet, confusing, laughable, and flattering (if I'm being totally honest) that Damian thought I'd come back to, uh, chill. Before I had to let him down, though, a familiar voice rang out across the clearing.

"Damian." In the bleached half-light, Jen looked older too: her movements stiff, her face lined, that long (almost distended) jaw set hard. Some of that, I thought, was anger, not age. "Where have you been?"

Damian folded his arms, and he didn't quite look at Jen. "Could you keep your voice down—"

"I've been looking for you all morning."

Instead of answering, Damian shot me a look—an appeal for sympathy, like he and I were in this together, and wasn't she being so unreasonable. The kind of look that stops being cute around age twelve.

"Grab some gloves and get to work," Jen said.

"Yeah," Damian said. "We're talking. I'll do it in a minute—"

"Not in a minute. Right now. That's the deal—you crash here, you work." A beat later, she shouted, "Go!"

Damian sent me one last, long-suffering look—this one tinged with a sulk—and said, "Hit me up before you leave." He brushed past Jen and headed toward the row of cabins. It wasn't quite a challenge, and it wasn't quite aggression, but it came close, and for a moment, rage lit up Jen's face.

Then she shut it down, and when she turned to me, her expression was neutral again. "You're Bobby's friend."

I nodded.

"Not to be rude, but I've got a lot going on this morning. Do you need something?"

"What happened?"

Jen pushed a hand through her boyishly short hair. She let out a breath slowly. "That nut job got in here last night. Ali Rivas—heard of her? Broke every window she could reach. And the cameras weren't working, of course, the one night I need them to work."

"The cameras weren't working?"

She started to shake her head, and then she looked at me more closely. "Is there something I can help you with?"

"Maybe. This is kind of weird, but—well, I'm the one who found, uh, Gerry last night." And then inspiration struck. "I'm kind of having a hard time, you know, processing."

"Oh. God. I'm so sorry."

"Yeah, he made a pass at me, and then, well, you know what happened with Bobby, and—I'm just feeling really messed up, I guess."

"I'm sorry," Jen said again. "He could get like that sometimes. I told the guys who were staying here not to let him get them alone."

"I thought the camp wasn't open. Actually, I don't really understand what's going on—why have the surf competition if the camp won't be ready until the spring?"

Jen flashed a smile. "Well, surfers don't really need much of an excuse to catch a wave and throw a party. The real answer, though, is that we've been hosting the camp—and the challenge—for years. But we've always run the camp out of a resort down the coast. Next year, we'll have our own place." She put her hands on her hips. "We would have, anyway. I don't know what's going on now that Gerry's…"

"From what you said, he seems kind of, I don't know, problematic as a business partner."

"You mean letting him walk around and prey on eighteen- and nineteen-year-olds? Yeah, I didn't exactly know what I was getting myself into. It's not like that's the kind of person I'd have picked."

"How'd you guys end up working together?"

"I'd been trying to get the camp going for a long time. I was eyeing this property, trying to work out the loan, and the next thing I knew, he swooped in and bought it out from under me. Part of that stupid planned community. I was so mad I showed up at his office and gave him a piece of my mind."

That wasn't what I remembered Gerry saying, but admittedly, I'd had other things on my mind. "And that worked?"

Something about Jen's shrug seemed amused. "I had a good deal lined up, and he cheated me out of it. I called him on it. Then he wanted to know about the camp, and I told him, and he seemed really supportive. I mean, I should have picked up on it then—you saw him, the way he dyed his hair and that stupid goatee, the clothes, trying to look like he was thirty years younger. He had a reputation in Portland, you know. I asked some of the guys. They said he was on all the apps. Kind of a standing joke; everybody knew what he liked."

"He wasn't local?"

"Gerry? No. Like I said, Portland."

"What about you?"

She shook her head. "Grew up in California. I've been coming up here for the cold-water surfing for a long time. Then I started doing the camp in the fall. I would have made the move permanent once this place opened." Her fingers flexed and settled on her hips again. "I shouldn't be talking about it like it's over, but God, who knows?"

"Why would it be over?"

"Because he owns the land. Because he was putting up most of the money for the camp itself." Jen let out an unhappy little laugh. "Because he's the only reason this thing ever got off the ground in the first place."

"You were partners, then?"

Jen nodded, but she didn't seem to have heard me.

"But it was your idea, right? I mean, you must have been the majority shareholder, or however you say it."

She started to nod again. Then she brought her head up and considered me. Her expression wasn't wary. It wasn't even defensive, not exactly. But it was...closed, I guess, in a way it hadn't been before.

I decided to risk a lie. "The reason I ask is I heard the cops talking about an argument you guys had. About money, right?"

The caution in her expression evaporated in a flash of heat. "No, not about money. About his stupid idea to turn this into a daycare. Listen, I like working with kids. But this is my surf camp. It's not an amenity for his planned community. It doesn't matter whose name is on the paperwork." She drew a breath. "Who said we were having an argument?"

I didn't want to get into a game of he said-she said, mostly because I had no idea who had said anything, so I said, "How'd he get up there, anyway?"

"What?"

"On the cliff. Did anyone see him after, you know, that stuff with Bobby?"

Jen shifted her weight. "I don't get why you're so interested."

Genius struck again. "Oh, I was just thinking out loud, I guess. Wondering about liability, you know—if the family might sue because the surf camp was negligent."

"That's ridiculous! He was so drunk he could barely stand up—you saw him staggering out of here. And I wasn't his babysitter. You walk that way—" She pointed toward the ocean. "—and you end up right at the cliffs. Flat ground, an easy walk. It's only a few hundred yards."

I tried to construct a mental map. That made sense—the route I'd taken the night before, when I'd been following Deputy Bobby, had definitely taken me downhill until I reached the beach. The route had also curved a fair bit, following the natural slope of the ground. It made sense that it would have taken me longer to go down to the beach and then along the bluffs to reach the spot where Gerry had fallen; Gerry, on the other hand, could have gotten there in a few minutes (depending on how many times he stumbled along the way, I guess).

"Do you mind if I take a look?"

Her eyes widened; apparently, she hadn't been expecting that. "Yeah, I do, actually."

"Why?"

"Because a man died out there."

"Technically, he died on the beach, not on the cliff."

"Are you kidding me?"

"I just need a quick look. I promise I won't disturb anything."

"No!" She seemed to be trying to think of a reason because then she said, "The deputies were out there all night. You might mess something up."

"But they already left," I said. "Which means they're done."

I took a step in the direction she pointed, and she moved into my path. "You can't go out there. It's like you said: the cliffs are dangerous, and what if the camp is liable? I don't want to be on the hook for anybody else."

"I'll sign a waiver."

When I tried to step around her again, she caught my arm. She was strong—I'd known she was strong, but she was even stronger than she looked. "I think you should leave." She released me and stepped back, but she was still in my way. She wouldn't quite meet my eyes as she said, "I'm sorry about what happened to you, but I don't feel comfortable letting you wander around out there."

I got back in the Jeep and left, but instead of going back to the state highway, I took the first turn I came to. It led me south, in the general direction of Klikamuks Head. The dirt roads weren't labeled, but fortunately, everybody who drove back this far was headed for the same place: the beach.

It took me fifteen minutes to find another route down to the water, and I parked on a square of flattened grass where a piece of driftwood had been laid like a parking stop. Beaches in Oregon—every inch of coastline, in fact—were public property, which meant that while Jen might have the authority to kick me out of the surf camp (although I wasn't sure about that, since Gerry had been the owner), she couldn't keep me off the beach.

When I got out of the Jeep, the sound of the surf met me, and a stiff breeze raked my hair. Big, white-capped waves tumbled and broke out on the water. I shivered; the canvas jacket, I decided, definitely wasn't going to cut it.

I worked my way up the beach as quickly as I could, sticking to the firmer sand near the waterline and setting a pace that balanced speed and, well, my current level of conditioning. The wind made a high-pitched noise, and when it faded, even for a moment, the detritus of shells crunched underfoot. I'd read about the bottom of the ocean. Marine snow, that's what they called it: the powdery blizzard of bone dust left by millions—billions—of deaths. The day had a crushed, grayish-white glow. Still no shadows.

It was faster going this time. I passed the lifeguard tower and the racks of drying wetsuits, the surfboards lined up at attention. Nobody was out on the water today. It'd be nice to think they were grieving Gerry—it'd be nice to think somebody was grieving him, anyway. But I had a feeling this had more to do with the surf conditions, and possibly with Jen, than it did with anything else.

When I reached the bluffs, I cut across the sand and found a path—barely more than a cut in the rocky face—I could scramble up. Stone gave back the sound of my breathing, which, admittedly, was starting to sound a little labored. I pushed my way through scrub, the brush stiff and rustling. A few thorns caught the backs of my hands. Then the bushes and tall grass gave way to hemlock and pine, and I crested the rise.

As I made my way to the cliff where Gerry had fallen, the wind rose, and over the slap of the waves came the creak and protest of the branches above me. He'd come out here at night, I thought. Drunk. Maybe he'd wanted to see the water. I glanced behind me; the nearest outbuilding of the camp couldn't have been more than a couple hundred yards, which meant Jen had been telling the truth. Maybe he'd just wanted some privacy, time to collect the shreds of his dignity, not unlike Deputy Bobby. Or maybe, like a boy, he'd wanted to pee off a cliff.

Not fell, a part of my brain revised. Was pushed.

But—had he been pushed? My memory of finding Gerry was a welter of impressions: the swash running over my feet, the spray on the side of my face, the heat of a held breath in my chest. In the dark, Gerry had been nothing more than a jumble of body parts. And while I had been sure, earlier, that I'd seen a shadow above me, now that I stood here, it seemed...well, unlikely was the politest way to put it. The cliff was higher than I realized. And there'd only been weak, ambient light. It could have been a trick of my eyes. It could have been a drop of water on my glasses.

Adjusting my glasses now, I pushed through the last line of hemlocks to reach the edge of the cliff. A stiff gale met me, braced me, howled in my face. I stared down at the lip of ground that ran until the drop: a few weeds, and then nothing but small stones and pebbles, basically gravel. No sign of a footprint. No disturbance to suggest a man had ever stood here—much less that he had struggled here and been forced to his death. Closer to the trees there was a thin layer of soil, but even that looked clear of any possible impression. I turned on the flashlight on my phone and raked the light, trying to catch a hint of some depression or other irregularity to suggest Gerry had walked here, stood here, hell, that he'd ever even been here.

Nothing but the marks I'd made.

I gave up and started back the way I'd come. I tried to replay the events of the night: finding Gerry's body, the stunned realization of what I'd stumbled across, and then—had it been movement? Had something at the edge of my vision drawn my attention, and that's why I'd looked up? Or had it been automatic, instinctual: mapping his fall in reverse, my brain still trying to understand what had happened. I eased my way down the steep path, and with every step, I was less certain I'd seen what I thought I'd seen. If there had been something to see, the professionals would have found it. And I'd just seen with my own eyes, there was nothing—

There was nothing to see.

My heart started to beat a little faster. My brain whirred. I was so caught up in my thoughts that I skidded-slipped-slid the last few yards to the bottom of the bluff. There'd been nothing to see up there. Even though gravel and damp soil should have taken some kind of print. Which meant—

I hadn't been paying attention. As I dropped down from the rocky chute I'd been following, I caught a glimpse of movement too late. A hand grabbed me and spun me in a circle.

I reared back, fighting to pull free. And then I stopped and stared at Deputy Bobby.

"What is wrong with you?" I asked. (It was more of a shout.) "You almost gave me a heart attack!"

Deputy Bobby was dressed in a dark green rain jacket, dark jeans, and his old hiking boots. With the hood up, and the day's skeletal light, the effect was like camouflage. No, my brain told me as it caught up. It *was* camouflage. Because Deputy Bobby was out here sneaking.

He still hadn't said anything, but I recognized the tension in his jaw, the way he set himself, arms folded across his chest. I'd only made Deputy Bobby mad a few times, and it was never a fun experience.

"You scared me," I said in a milder voice. "I thought—" I thought the killer had gotten me, I almost said, but I was saving that line for when I was asked to star in a local production of *Nancy Drew and the Scary Deputy.* "I thought I was in trouble."

"Funny you should say that," Deputy Bobby said.

CHAPTER 5

Deputy Bobby chivvied me along the beach. He didn't push. He didn't prod. I got the impression that he was battling a powerful urge to take me by the arm and haul me along like we were headed to the principal's office, but he somehow managed to keep his hands to himself. He didn't need to do any of that; all he had to do was point, and I scooted right along.

But when we approached the lifeguard tower, Deputy Bobby made a sharp noise and cocked his head, and I realized he meant I was supposed to turn. Tower was a misleading description—it was more like a small hut or cabin built on a metal frame. A shelter, I guess. The shelter was a wooden structure that had probably, one day in the distant past, been a beautiful shade of light blue. The paint was the color of a dead pigeon now, with a molted look where large strips had peeled away. It had big windows behind wooden shutters, deep eaves, and what appeared to be an observation deck on top. A ramp led up to the tower, with an old metal bucket chained to the post at the bottom. Deputy Bobby made that noise again, and I followed the ramp.

"What's happening?" I asked when I reached the shelter.

Deputy Bobby stepped past me. He did something to the door, and the hinges screeched as it swung open. Inside, the shelter was dark, and a faint, musty odor like wet wood and mildew wafted out.

"I want to know—"

"Go inside," Deputy Bobby said, "or you're going to get arrested."

I wasn't sure he'd arrest me, not really. But I wasn't sure he wouldn't either.

Inside, that odor was stronger. It wasn't entirely unpleasant. The shelter had a simple layout: a storage area with hooks and lockers, where lifeguards must have stored gear and supplies; an ancient desk, with a discolored spot to suggest where once, I suspected, a two-way radio had been bolted; in the corner, a dusty cooler with the name GUS spelled out in duct tape on one side; and a ladder that led up to the observation deck. A bare light bulb hung overhead, but it was off, and with the shutters closed against the day's bone-white light, the inside of the shelter was dark.

Deputy Bobby stepped in behind me and shut the door. Then it was *really* dark. And really quiet. Deputy Bobby's breathing wasn't exactly agitated. But it wasn't relaxed, either. My own breathing probably sounded like Road Runner after giving Coyote a run for his money. Deputy Bobby's silhouette moved slightly—shifting his weight, I thought. Sand rasped and crunched underfoot.

"I have every right to be up there," I said. It was important to start strong—and to avoid the slightly more complicated question of if I actually did have *every* right, or if I might have, just a wee bit, been doing some light trespassing. "And you should be happy—"

"I should be happy?"

The thing about Deputy Bobby is that he rarely raised his voice. His tone didn't even change that much. If you didn't know him very well, you could have heard that question and thought it was the same way somebody would have asked if he should take out the trash, or if he should stop and pick up groceries on the way home. If you did know him, though—

"Okay, I understand you're upset, but—"

"Be quiet."

"—I actually think the sheriff is making a big mistake—"

Deputy Bobby held up his hand. "Stop."

"—and if you'll let me explain—"

"Dash." His voice was a low crack. "Stop talking."

The sting came a moment later: a flush rising in my face, an airiness in my head. I thought of the night before. How I'd stood there, letting Gerry paw at me. Well, being paralyzed by my own anxiety once a week seemed like more than enough, so I started for the door.

"Hold on—" Deputy Bobby began.

I shook my head.

He still hadn't moved, but that didn't matter. He wouldn't stop me; I knew him well enough for that.

And then my foot came down on something hard and round. A marble—that was my one, instantaneous thought before my foot flew out from under me, and I fell.

Deputy Bobby caught me, of course. It probably wasn't easy, since I'm a few inches taller than him, and Indira has cookbook after cookbook of just cakes. But Deputy Bobby was also very strong. I was aware of that strength as my brain caught up with my body: the powerful lines of his arms wrapped around me; the hint of saltwater and sweat and a clean, masculine fragrance that was probably his deodorant; the warmth of him. I hadn't realized, until right then, how cold I was.

"Let me—" I began.

"Please be quiet," he whispered.

And then the sounds filtered through the chaos inside my head: voices—indistinct, but, I thought, male; the tread of footsteps through sand; the crackle of a radio.

I could feel Deputy Bobby's question. My face was still pressed into his shoulder, but I nodded.

The voices came closer, although the words remained indistinct. Deputy Bobby tensed. His whole body seemed like it was worked in iron, and I was suddenly, dangerously aware of him, like the flicker of a flame inside me, a fire that was still trying to catch. I thought maybe it would be a good idea (for everybody) if I put a little distance between us, but when I tried to move, Deputy Bobby let out a vexed breath and tightened his grip.

Oh. My. God.

After what must have been an eternity, the voices moved back the way they had come. Deputy Bobby didn't relax until the rolling thunder of the waves had completely swallowed them. Then he whispered, "I'm going to let you down now."

I nodded into his shoulder again, and he eased me to the floor. Aside from being a bit sandy, the floorboards were smooth from decades of use. I was having a hard time looking Deputy Bobby in the face, so I focused on his knees and said, "Thanks. I didn't—I didn't understand why you were telling me to be quiet." And then I felt like I had to add, "Obviously."

And in a tone that could have meant anything, he said, "Obviously."

He sat crisscross opposite me. The gloom of the shelter made it hard to pick out the expression on his face. Then a smile gleamed, and he held up something that glinted in the weak light. He pressed it into my hand, his fingers sparking against mine and then gone again. Whatever it was, it was cool and round and felt like glass.

"A marble?" I said, which was still the only thing I could come up with, even though I could tell this was too big to be one.

"Japanese fishing float." His tone still could have meant anything. "They used them to keep the tops of their nets afloat."

"Oh." And because that had to be the lamest mouth-sound any mouth had ever mouthed, I managed to top myself by saying, "Um."

For some reason, that made Deputy Bobby laugh, and his real grin—the big, goofy one—flashed out.

"Well, I'm still processing!"

That made him laugh harder. He had a nice laugh; it wasn't something I heard often. I decided the best, most mature, most adult response to that sound, which I could never get enough of, was to be slightly offended.

"Thanks, I guess," I said. "Were those guys from the surf camp?"

"Those were deputies."

"Because Jen called them and said I was trespassing."

"You *were* trespassing."

"Whose side are you on here? Hey, wait! Does that mean you weren't going to arrest me?"

"What?"

"When we got here." I gestured to the door. "You said, 'Get inside, or I'll arrest your skinny white butt right now.'"

"I never said that. And of course I wouldn't arrest you." He considered that. "Have you paid all your parking tickets?"

"Rude!"

"What were you doing on that cliff?"

"Inspecting. Investigating. Detecting."

"Like Will Gower?" he asked drily.

Definitely like Will Gower, I thought, although I wasn't going to give him the satisfaction of an answer. Will Gower didn't take guff from anybody. He was a cynical private investigator with a bad case of white knight syndrome. He was an honest cop who nevertheless played by his own rules. In one disastrous attempt, he'd been a whalebone corsetier with a thirst for revenge (and whale bones). (A corsetier, by the way, is a person who makes corsets, which, let me tell you, typing *Person who makes corsets profession* into Google was one of the more surreal experiences of my life.)

"Do you know what I found up there?" I asked.

"It doesn't matter what you found up there," Deputy Bobby said, "because you're not a law enforcement officer, and you're certainly not part of this investigation, and I'm sure, because you're a smart young man—"

"You're three years older than me, not thirty-three."

"—you would never do something so foolish as to be snooping."

"First, I object to the term snooping—"

"Dash."

"Nothing! There was nothing up there. No footprints. No scuffs. Nothing. There's soft soil. There's bare stone. There's a stretch of gravel. It should have been easy to see where Gerry had been—an impression in the dirt, or a print he tracked onto the stone, or even just displaced gravel to show where he'd stepped. But there's nothing!"

Deputy Bobby didn't say anything.

"Someone covered it up!"

Deputy Bobby still didn't say anything.

"That proves it's a murder, see? Gerry couldn't have covered his own tracks because he fell. So, it had to be the killer, and they were so scared about leaving evidence behind that they overcorrected and wiped out any sign at all."

"Maybe the ground wasn't soft enough to take an impression. Maybe it wasn't muddy enough to leave a track on the stone. Maybe the gravel was spread too thin."

"Maybe. But I checked, and I left prints."

Nothing changed in Deputy Bobby's face. And that didn't make any sense because even though Deputy Bobby was on leave—was, basically, already out of the sheriff's office—Deputy Bobby had strong opinions about right and wrong. In fact, he—

My jaw dropped. "What the heck?"

(Not exactly—use your imagination.)

Deputy Bobby arched his eyebrows, but a hint of uncertainty underlay his usual even keel.

"You think he was murdered too!" Glee made my voice rise. "You think I'm right!"

"I think we should let law enforcement—"

"You do! You think he was murdered! That's why you're out here sneaking around like—like Rambo!"

"Like Rambo?"

"Oh no, don't you dare get me off track. I want answers."

"Where was this attitude when Keme skipped school last week?"

"Deputy Bobby!"

He winced, and his smile was like a cracked mirror when he said, "Just Bobby, remember?"

I wanted to say something about that. I did. But instead, I said, "You do, don't you?"

He shrugged. But then he said, "I thought I saw someone." And then he gave me that broken smile again. "Besides you."

So, that answered one question: I *had* been following Deputy Bobby the night before. "But why didn't you stop when you found Gerry?"

"Because I know better than to walk along the base of a cliff where a rock could fall on my head. I cut up toward the bluffs; I was going back to the camp when I saw somebody up on the ridge." I opened my mouth, and he shook his head. "Just their silhouette—the clouds were breaking up, and they stood out against the sky. Otherwise, I never would have seen them."

"Did you tell the sheriff?"

Deputy Bobby had a very communicative look sometimes.

"Okay, but why didn't she believe you?"

"She did believe me. She's smart, and she's good at her job. But she's also in a situation where there's no evidence to suggest a murder."

"But—"

He held up a hand. "I know. And I'm not saying you're wrong. But outside of a Sherlock Holmes novel, the whole 'lack of evidence is evidence' thing isn't as compelling as you think."

I gave him an appraising glance. "Say something else about Sherlock Holmes."

The corner of his mouth twitched, but his voice was serious when he said, "Why are you doing this?"

Well, I thought, because it kind of seemed like the sheriff suspected you. But I said, "Because someone killed Gerry, and they're going to get away with it, and that's not right."

It was impossible to read the look on Deputy Bobby's face.

"So," I said, "I'm going to get my gat and throw iron and pump the killer full of lead."

"What?"

"I have an overdeveloped sense of justice from reading too much Chandler."

"Do you know, sometimes I have zero idea what you're saying?"

"I know. Your face is extra cute when you're trying to figure it out."

I heard what I said, ladies and gentlemen. And that was when I died. Angels wept as they carried me out of my body.

Somehow, my still shambling corpse managed to stammer, "Anyway, I think I know who did it. Or who *might* have done it, anyway. There's that guy, Nate, the one who's on the city council."

"The glorified used-car salesman?"

"You had to break up their fight at the beach, remember?"

"Murder's different from taking a swing at somebody."

"And there's that protester, the one who thinks everybody is building on sacred land."

"To be fair, she's not wrong about Gerry. The Confederated Tribes don't have any objection to events on the beach, but that new development is on an important ceremonial site."

"See what I mean? Maybe she and Nate were in on it together."

"Nate wasn't mad about a ceremonial site," Deputy Bobby said.

"What was he mad about?"

"I don't know, but I'll bet you a box of donuts that it had something to do with money."

"Like, you buy me a box of donuts if I'm right? And I buy you a box of donuts if you're right? But either way, we both get donuts because we're friends and we share?"

"If I win, you don't get to eat any donuts for a week."

"Oh God, no, that's a big pass."

"For one week, Dash?"

"Are you a monster? They're donuts!"

Some of the iron in his shoulders relaxed. He leaned against the desk. He wasn't wearing that awful, cracked-in-half smile; instead, he looked the way he did sometimes, when I said or did something particularly...Dashian. Like he didn't have any idea what to do, frankly. Like he'd found something new in the world. Like he might smile.

"I want you to leave this alone," he said in his earnest, Deputy Bobby way. "I understand that you want to see justice done. That's one of the things I—" He stopped. Swallowed. "That's admirable. But this is dangerous. I'll explain what you found to the sheriff."

"And she'll weigh it and consider it and decide I'm full of beans."

"Is that an expression?"

"And the killer will have more time to cover their tracks."

"Dash, a proper murder investigation takes manpower, resources—we don't have any of that."

The *we* sent a little thrill through me.

In true Deputy Bobby fashion, though, he managed to grind all the fun out of it when he continued, "I promise I'm not going to let this get swept under the rug, but I want you to promise me you'll leave it alone."

"No."

"Dash—"

"You're not a deputy anymore. Or you're on leave. Or whatever."

"I'm telling you that this is too dangerous, and I'm asking you—"

"And you're moving."

He sounded like he was struggling to control his voice. "I am asking you," he said again, "to promise me—"

"In a couple of weeks, you won't even be thinking about this case anymore. Gerry didn't mean anything to you, and you'll be busy with your new home and your new friends and your new life. You'll forget all about—" *Me* almost slipped out of my mouth. "—Hastings Rock."

"If I tell you I'm going to do something, I'm going to do it." His volume surged. "And it doesn't matter that I'm not a deputy anymore. And it doesn't matter that I'm moving, or that I didn't know Gerry, or that I'm going to be busy with other things. I'm saying this because I care about you! Because I want you to be safe! And for God's sake, Dash, I'm not going to forget you!"

The light dimmed inside the shelter like an eclipse. The wind rattled the shutters. Deputy Bobby stared at me, breathing hard.

I stared back. A prickle started in my eyes, but I refused to look away.

For another moment, we both stayed like that. Then Deputy Bobby sagged back. He slapped the side of the desk, and the clap filled the shelter's cramped space. I flinched and looked away.

The break of the waves filled the silence.

"I'm going to go," I said.

Deputy Bobby clasped his hands and rested his head on them. When I started to move, he didn't look up, but he did say, "Don't." It wasn't an order, not really. It was low. And it sounded like begging.

So, I didn't.

After several long heartbeats, Deputy Bobby took a ragged breath. "Can we talk about something?" He seemed to struggle, and then he added, "I just need a few minutes." The sound he made was a try at a laugh, but a bad one. "Anything, Dash. Please."

I didn't mean anything by it; it had been on my mind, that's all, and it was the first thing that popped out of my mouth. "Are you all packed?"

"God, please. Anything but that." He shifted slightly, as though trying to get more comfortable, but his head still didn't come up. "What about your story? The anthology. Tell me about that."

"How do you know about that?"

"West."

"Uh, it's going great."

Deputy Bobby laughed—croaked, really—but his head came up. His eyes were red, but dry. His knuckles had left livid spots where they'd pressed into his forehead.

"It's a disaster," I said. "I mean, my parents assume I can just polish up something I've been working on and send it over. I honestly think they believe that I—I don't know. That I write all the time, but I choose not to send it out, or I'm lazy, or something."

"You do write all the time."

"I sit at my computer. I type a few words. A lot more disappear. I call it the Case of the Vanishing Manuscript."

"Why don't you just type more words and not delete any?"

"God, wouldn't that be nice?"

"I'm serious: why don't you? It's just a story, Dash. You type one word. Then the next one." Something changed in his face. What I might, if Will Gower had seen it, have described as a hint of good-natured devilry. "'Begin at the beginning, and go on till you come to the end: then stop.'"

I wondered if my eyebrows could fly off my face. "Sherlock Holmes and Lewis Carroll in one conversation?"

He gave me that embarrassed half-smile and a one-shouldered shrug, but the question did seem sincere. From anybody else, I probably would have taken offense at the question. Scratch that: I would have gone into an icy rage, completely shut down, and retreated to Hemlock House to soothe myself with an abundance of snickerdoodles. But since it was Deputy Bobby, the question wasn't just sincere. It was earnest. And, unexpectedly, I found myself wanting to answer it.

"It's hard to put into words." A grin slanted across my mouth. "I guess that's my whole problem; everything is hard to put into words, which isn't ideal for a writer. I guess—it's like, I have this story in my head, and it's so good. I know it's good. And I'm not just saying that. I've read a lot. And what I've sent out, I've gotten good feedback on. I'm not going to be the next Bill Shakespeare, but I know I've got good stories to tell. And then I sit down to write, and it's like—it's like there's this blender in my gut, all these bright, shiny blades, and they start spinning as fast as they can. Everything I do seems wrong. And every time I do something wrong, I realize everything else is wrong too. And there's this part of me that thinks if I can fix just this one word and get it perfect, then I'll be able to get the next one. But instead, I putz around and make it worse, and then everything else is worse, and there's all that sharp metal whirling around inside me, all this light and glitter like teeth trying to eat me up, and—" I made a gesture with one hand. "Poof. The Case of the Vanishing Manuscript."

Deputy Bobby stared at me. He had eyes the color of burnished bronze, and his pupils were huge in the low light. He'd clasped his hands again, and his knuckles blanched under the pressure.

"It's hard to describe," I said. "My therapists—notice the plural—have suggested a lot of reasons. I mean, I'm a perfectionist, obviously. And there's a lot of pressure to perform because my parents are who they are. And I can't remember the term from the DSM, but I'm a diagnosable whack-a-doodle."

He still hadn't said anything. He didn't even seem to be breathing. I had a strange moment where I thought I remembered this—the way he'd seemed stunned, struck to silence by something. It had been with Hugo, I thought. Or when I'd been telling him about Hugo. And then the moment was gone, and I couldn't call it back.

"Anyway," I said into the stiffening silence, "please refer back to this conversation whenever you need a refresher on why I'm painfully single."

Deputy Bobby jolted, and his face changed as though he were suddenly seeing me again. He worked his jaw. And then, in a tone I couldn't decipher, he said, "Do you know what my dad said when I told him I was moving back to Portland with West?"

It was such a strange question, with such a yawning emptiness behind it, that I couldn't answer; the best I could do was shake my head.

"He asked how I was going to find an apartment." Deputy Bobby gave a jagged laugh. "And my mom said, 'Good, now you can be a doctor.'"

"Jeez."

He let his head fall back to thunk against the desk.

"I thought—" I stopped. "I mean, I just assumed you were going to be a police officer—"

"That would make sense," Deputy Bobby said, and the words had an unfamiliar edge, "wouldn't it?"

I thought about West, though. His anger. His fear that lay behind that anger. And, through the door that Deputy Bobby had cracked for me, if only for an instant, I saw a line of people behind West going a long way back in Deputy Bobby's life.

"I didn't mean to bring that up," Deputy Bobby said. "My point was—I guess, parents are hard. I get that." Then he gave me a sideways smile. "Even if they're not famous."

"The famous part is actually amazing. I go to fabulous parties with the Kardashians, and everything I own is made out of diamonds—"

"Even your underwear?"

"—and I'm offended you never once asked for my autograph."

I got the goofy grin. Just for a moment. "I'm sorry I raised my voice."

"I'm sorry I, uh, tapped into a strong passive-aggressive ley line."

"You didn't have any friends when you were a kid, did you?"

"Deputy Bobby!" But I was grinning.

"It's like one thing after another that makes zero sense when it comes out of your mouth."

I was still trying to tamp down my grin—and working on my comeback, obviously—when Deputy Bobby stood. He held out a hand, and I let him help me to my feet. He had a nice hand, by the way. Strong. Defined. Solid. And it was funny, I thought, how you could know right away whether your hand would fit just right with someone else's. (Tragic backstory reveal: my hand did not fit just right with Shawn Laffleur's during the 6:35 p.m. screening of 2003's *Pirates of the Caribbean: The Curse of the Black Pearl*. He had popcorn fingers, and he gripped me way too hard. But we still made out anyway.)

"You're not going to let this go, are you?" Deputy Bobby asked.

"Definitely not. I'm going to call all my friends and make them fly out here to prove I was popular."

Deputy Bobby straightened my jacket for me. And then he gave me a look.

"It's not right," I said. "It wouldn't be right."

He nodded. "So, as soon as you're out of my sight, let me guess—you're going to break into Gerry's beach house?"

"I actually didn't know he had a beach house. Also, this feels like entrapment."

"Maybe I should just arrest you right now," he murmured.

"West would certainly have opinions if he found out you had plans to handcuff me."

Deputy Bobby didn't say anything to that. But, for an instant, his eyes came up to mine, and his smile wasn't goofy at all. It was slow and small and sure, and I was suddenly painfully aware of his fingers still holding my lapels, of how close we were standing, of the cramped shelter, of the faint hint of that clean, masculine scent. If you've ever had a firework go off inside you—in a very, very, very good way—you know what I'm talking about.

"I've decided to enter a monastery," I said.

For one last heartbeat, I got that other smile, the one I'd never seen before. The one with promises. And then Deputy Bobby released my jacket, stepped back, and said, "That would be a waste."

I could still feel him, though. The echo of him.

He turned for the door and said, "Let's go."

"Oh," I managed to say. "You're going with me now?"

"If you're going to be a smart aleck about this," he said as he stepped outside, "I'll lend Fox and Keme my handcuffs."

CHAPTER 6

Deputy Bobby insisted we wait until dark before breaking into Gerry Webb's beach house, but he also didn't trust me not to go without him, which meant we had to kill time together. We got lunch at the Otter Slide. And then we stopped by the library to pick up some books (for me). And then Deputy Bobby needed one of those special TV boxes to pack up his TV. As we ran errands, I tried to do some light cyberstalking of Gerry, but I didn't get far. Deputy Bobby kept saying interesting things. And I kept saying funny things. (At least, I thought they were funny; Deputy Bobby just got that little furrow between his eyebrows and stared at me earnestly, waiting for clarification.) And it was all so...good.

Faster than I expected, dark settled over Hastings Rock. Gerry Webb's beach house was just on the north side of the bay—not far from the beach where the surfing competition had been held. It was hard to believe that had only been the day before; it felt like years. The house was set back on the lot, with privacy hedges on either side to screen out the neighbors, and the lawn and flower beds had a tidy look that suggested professional landscaping at the end of the season. The design of the house itself seemed to be based on a farmhouse aesthetic, built long and low with a gable roof. But some diagnosable whack-a-doodle had added their own twist on things—a sharp peak to the roofline above the entryway, for example, or the garages (yes, two), which had been built skinny and tall, the way a little kid might draw them. The general effect, I decided, was as if a six-year-old had tried to build a barn out of Legos.

The street—worn-down asphalt crumbling at the shoulders—didn't look like it got much traffic, but Deputy Bobby made me drive to the end of the block. I parked, and Deputy Bobby said, "Hang here for a minute while I check it out."

"Nice try."

He gave me his professional-grade deputy stare, but maybe being on leave made it less effective. I unbuckled my seat belt and slid out of the Jeep.

As I made my way down the street, Deputy Bobby's steps crunched the broken asphalt behind me. When he caught up, he had a little furrow between his eyebrows. "It might not be safe."

"It's cute, Deputy Bobby." There was that word again. "And I appreciate it. But I know what's going to happen. You're going to search the whole house while I sit in the Jeep playing Wizard Princess on my phone—"

"What is Wizard Princess?"

"How are you a person? What do you do all day—lift heavy things, catch bad guys, and surf? Don't you ever just scroll Instagram until your eyes fall out of your face and play games that make lots of awesome sounds and you have to tap the screen really fast?"

He seemed to give this serious—and in my opinion, undue— consideration. Finally he said, "I like Scrabble."

"Scrabble is literally the worst game ever! Do you know what it's like to have writer's block and play Scrabble?"

"I know this is my first time breaking and entering, but honestly, I thought it would involve significantly less yelling."

I refused to acknowledge that statement.

When we got to the house, Deputy Bobby made a straight line to the front porch. I trailed after him. The breeze off the ocean stirred the hedges, and the rustle of leaves swallowed the sound of our steps. I glanced left and right, but I couldn't make out anything on the other side of the boxwood. I hoped it worked the other way as well—we were exposed to the street, but I was more worried about a nosy neighbor spotting us and wondering why we were, uh, ingressing.

Deputy Bobby stood on the porch, considering the door. Off in the distance, wind chimes rang softly. The windows of the house were dark, and in the day's half-tone light, it was impossible to see inside beyond a few feet—I glimpsed an uncomfortable-looking bench, the edge of a glass coffee table, and a lamp that looked like someone had made it by using tin snips on a can of tuna.

"We should try the garage," I said. "I watched a YouTube video about how to use a plastic water bottle and—wait, do you have a pair of tin snips?"

Deputy Bobby said, "Hmm," the way I sometimes did to Millie.

"Are we going to pick the lock?"

Deputy Bobby said, "Maybe," in a way that I'd definitely said to Millie before.

"I could try to pick it," I said, "but we'd have to go back to Hemlock House for my picks. Also, I'm not very good. Also, I know you're going to think I'm making this up to get rid of you, but I have to admit I'd feel a certain amount of, er, performance anxiety if you were just standing there watching me, and—what are you doing?"

Without answering, Deputy Bobby crossed the porch to a decorative ceramic bird that perched on a three-legged table. He lifted the bird, turned it over to expose a hole in the base, and gave the bird a few experimental shakes. Something metallic rattled inside, and a moment later, a key tumbled out. Deputy Bobby caught it, set the ceramic bird back in its place, and gave me a look.

"You knew that was there," I said.

He might have been smiling.

"That's impossible," I said. "That couldn't have just been a guess."

With a tiny shrug, he turned to the door.

The key went in smoothly, of course, and a moment later, we stepped into the house.

Inside, the décor appeared to be farmhouse meets industrial chic meets zebra. Lots of earth tones. Lots of monochromatic "warmth." Matte black finishes on exposed metal. A zigzagging geometric pattern on one wall. On another, just to keep things interesting, a Tommy Bahama-inspired tropical wallpaper. The whole thing suggested that an interior designer had been given free rein and a blank check. It also suggested, quite possibly, that the interior designer had been working with his or her eyes closed.

We stood in an entry hall with a door on our left and a flight of stairs on our right. Ahead of us, the entry hall flowed into a great room, at the far end of which a wall of windows looked out on the ocean. The great room was combined, in true open-concept fashion, with a big, beautiful kitchen.

Deputy Bobby called out, "Hello?"

I jumped out of my skin.

No one answered, and Deputy Bobby might—*might*—have been smiling again. "Just checking."

"What is wrong with you?"

"What?"

"Can you just not be so—so Deputy Bobby for, like, five seconds?"

He was definitely smiling. I just couldn't quite see it.

Before I had to murder him—and then get dragged into the tiresome process of disposing of the body, cleaning up the crime scene, and *then* continuing an already frustrating investigation—I moved over to the stairs and went up to the first landing. From there, I could see that the stairs continued into a large, open loft with—

"What kind of idiot puts a grand piano in a loft?" I asked.

"One with plenty of money," Deputy Bobby said.

When I got back to the entry hall, the door across from me was open, and Deputy Bobby stood inside what appeared to be Gerry's office, where the theme was urban cowboy: a big, masculine desk; nifty pens in a mug that said WORLD'S BEST DADDY (which I hoped to God was a joke); lots of aerial photography on the walls that, after a moment, I took to be some of Gerry's development projects. A cowhide rug covered the floor. A steer skull hung above the desk. He even had a taxidermy vulture (a little on the nose, maybe) that would have fit in perfectly at Hemlock House. Large windows looked out on the lawn and the street—which, I was relieved to note, appeared to be as sleepy as it had seemed.

Deputy Bobby already had on a pair of disposable gloves, and he began opening desk drawers.

"How do you have gloves?" I asked. "Are you always prepared for potential burgling?"

"Yes."

I stared at him. It's an interesting sensation, when you can literally feel your blood pressure rising.

"No," I said. "You're not."

He made a noise that was neither agreement nor disagreement or, really, anything except acknowledgment. And he kept searching.

I wondered what the policy was on screaming during a B&E. Somehow, though, I managed to keep myself at a strangled whisper: "What is happening?"

"You're being a smart aleck," he said as he opened another drawer, "and I'm driving you crazy."

I decided now was a good time to search somewhere else before there was murdering (see above).

Since Deputy Bobby hadn't offered to share his disposable gloves (where had he gotten them? and how? and when? and, most importantly, *how?*), I went to the kitchen first and checked under the sink. I found a few cleaning supplies, but no gloves. I had better luck in the pantry—a brand new box of nitrile gloves. I snapped on a pair and went to work.

I started in the bedroom. Unlike the rest of the house, this room actually looked lived in: a half-empty (yes, that's the kind of person I am) glass of water on the nightstand; a jumble of charging cables; a box of tissues that I hoped were for allergies; even a leather tray that held jewelry. It wasn't anything expensive, and honestly, it all looked like it was from the Trying Too Hard to Look Young school of fashion—leather bracelets, a silver chain, even an honest-to-God puka shell necklace.

It took me about zero-point-five seconds to find something interesting: on the unmade bed, half-covered by a pillow, was a laptop.

I picked it up and opened it, expecting a password prompt, but instead, I found myself staring at the computer's desktop. Maybe it hadn't shut all the way. Maybe he'd turned off the auto-lock feature. Maybe Gerry had disabled the password in general. Whatever the reason, it felt like a real don't-look-a-gift-horse-in-the-mouth situation, and I took the laptop to sit at the kitchen island.

I started with Gerry's emails, but there wasn't anything interesting there—it all appeared to be about work. I paused to examine some of the emails about the Hastings Rock development, but they were all about permits and contractors and designs and plans. If there was something nefarious in there, it was buried deep enough that I didn't recognize it.

Since his email had been a dead end, I tried his browser next. The thing about people who don't bother locking their computers? They also, apparently, don't bother erasing their search histories. Surprise, surprise, a lot of Gerry's searches had been about work. It looked like he'd been researching Hastings Rock's municipal codes—although surely he had someone he paid to do things like that.

Other items in the search history were clearly more personal—in keeping with the tray of Yes-I-Have-Gray-Chest-Hairs-But-I'm-Still-Cool jewelry. For example, he'd apparently been interested in branching out and trying some new hair dyes. (Perhaps something, this time, that didn't look like someone might have used it to paint a mule's tail.) Facial creams. Retinols. Retinoids.

Somatotropin (that was a new one for me, and I had to look it up). So many—so, so many—pages about Botox.

And then, in the midst of the list of Ways to Stay Young, there was a single search for Oregon truancy laws. Below that were two more entries—Oregon statutes on luring a minor and solicitation of a minor.

I grabbed the laptop and headed to the office.

Deputy Bobby was still working on the desk, and he glanced up as I stepped inside.

"So, Gerry liked young guys, right?" I said.

"You're not that young."

"I'm sorry, what was that?"

Deputy Bobby stopped his search. "Uh."

"I must have misheard you."

"You did. You misheard me. I was saying—"

"No, just stop before you make it worse." I showed him the search results. "Look at what he's been reading about. I mean, I know Jen said he likes young guys, but I didn't think she meant, you know, this."

With a frown, Deputy Bobby shook his head.

"Does this change things?" I asked. "Do we need to try to figure out who he's been seeing? Maybe this is revenge."

"Maybe," Deputy Bobby said. He left the desk and started removing photos from the wall, checking behind them before he replaced them again. With his back to me, he said, "You know Damian has an arrest record."

"What?"

"Damian."

"Okay," I said slowly. "For what? Did he go to jail?"

"His record doesn't show a conviction."

"So, you think he did this?" I did remember—vaguely, because at the time, my focus had been elsewhere—catching a glimpse of Damian's face when Gerry had been trying to grope me. Angry; in fact, he looked like he'd been furious.

Before I could share that memory, though, Deputy Bobby said, "No. I just thought you should know."

I opened my mouth to ask why he thought I needed to know that, at some point in his life, Damian had been arrested. And then it landed.

"Are you trying to tell me to stay away from him?"

I meant for it to sound light, joking. It didn't.

Deputy Bobby's shoulders tightened as he moved to the next photo.

"How did you even find that out?" I asked. My tone was still off, but I couldn't seem to get it back on track. "You're on leave."

"I just thought—"

"How?"

His hands fell to his sides. He stood very still. "Salk."

"You talked to another deputy about my—my romantic life?" I tried to stop there, but more words burst out of me. "I didn't even go out with him. He flirted with me. He seems sweet."

"Yeah, he seems sweet, and he's got an arrest record. That's important information, considering—"

He stopped himself, but not fast enough.

"Considering what?" I asked.

"Considering—"

I cut him off. "Considering I have terrible judgment when it comes to men? Considering I'm a complete idiot about relationships? Considering I don't know how to take care of myself?"

"I just want you to be safe." He still wasn't looking at me. I wanted to see his face; his voice sounded like someone trying desperately to stay calm. "And I was only checking—I didn't say any of those things."

"But you thought them, didn't you? I don't need you to be my chaperone, Bobby. Or my big brother. Or whatever you think this is."

"I think I'm your friend."

"Yeah, you're my friend, but God, Bobby, that is so invasive. How do you not see that?"

Whatever control he'd had must have slipped; the raw edge of his anger surfaced the way it had in the lifeguard tower. He moved to the next photo, his movements jerky and uncoordinated as he reached to take it down. "It was for sexual assault." He yanked the photo from the wall. "In case it matters."

I opened my mouth to say something, but then I saw what had been hidden behind the photo: a wall safe.

Deputy Bobby stared at it too. Then, slowly, he set down the photo. He inspected the lock and said, "It takes a key, not a combination."

I wanted to—well, to my surprise, I wanted to fight some more. But somehow, I managed to make my voice sound semi-sane as I said, "Maybe it's on Gerry's keyring. The sheriff could get it from the medical examiner, I guess, but first we'd have to convince her that, you know, Gerry was murdered."

Deputy Bobby nodded. He still hadn't looked at me.

"We could try to pick it," I said. "Do some research on this model and see if it's pickable, anyway. Or drill it out—I bet we could rent whatever we need. Heck, we could probably cut the door off with a torch."

After another moment of studying the safe door, Deputy Bobby moved over to the desk. He opened the central drawer and drew out a handful of loose keys. The first one he tried opened the safe, of course.

I couldn't help it: I said, "You have got to be kidding me."

Deputy Bobby glanced at me, and there was something so…hurt in his face that I had a hard time recapturing my anger.

I dredged up a small smile. "It was bad enough with the bird."

After a moment, Deputy Bobby smiled back. A tiny one. Microscopic, even. Maybe not even a smile, not really, but—but a question that was like a smile. My smile got a little bigger in answer, and his shoulders relaxed. And then he had to be perfectly, quintessentially Deputy Bobby, and he shrugged.

Even though that moment seemed to have defused the tension between us, neither of us spoke as Deputy Bobby withdrew a stack of files from the safe. He set them on the desk where we could both see them, and then we began to examine each one. Most of the documents were financial papers—things that you'd expect to find. Gerry's will (I took pictures of that), brokerage reports, account statements, even a few deeds.

Near the bottom of the stack, though, were folders. Lots of folders. And on each folder, there was a name. I took photos of everything, as quickly as I could,

Then I stopped. Because the name on the next folder was mine.

"Dash—" Deputy Bobby tried.

I flipped open the folder. Inside were photos. Photos of Hemlock House. Photos of me—taken through the open windows, when I'd been inside Hemlock House, unaware that anyone might be photographing me. Photos of Keme, too. Keme, with his long dark hair tucked behind his ears, in nothing but swim trunks. Keme and I on the sofa, sitting close together because we were playing Xbox. Keme and I—for a moment, I didn't understand the photo. We were on the floor, tangled together. My arms were wrapped around Keme's bare back.

I took several deep breaths. They didn't help.

Deputy Bobby was still looking at the photos.

"We went swimming," I said. "And then we came back and played video games. And I beat him, and he tackled me—it was silly." I thought back to those search results on Gerry's computer: truancy, luring a minor, solicitation of a minor. And then these photos of me and Keme, making it look like—I had to put my hand on the desk because I felt like I was starting to tip over. Somehow I managed to say, "We were wrestling."

Deputy Bobby threw me a quick look, and he must have known the right thing to say because he said, "I know, Dash. I know. It's okay."

But it wasn't okay. Gerry—or someone Gerry had hired—had taken those pictures. Gerry had kept those pictures. Gerry had—

"Shoot," Deputy Bobby said. (But the four-letter version.)

The tension in his voice broke through the cloud of my thoughts, and I followed his gaze. On the sleepy street that never had any traffic, a sheriff's office cruiser had just pulled up in front of the house.

"Come on," Deputy Bobby said.

I grabbed my folder.

"Dash—"

"No," I said. "No."

Frustration twisted Deputy Bobby's features, but he nodded and took me by the arm. I wanted to tell him I didn't need it, but the truth was, it was nice; my whole body felt strangely bloodless, and I had the impression that if Deputy Bobby let go of me, I'd just puddle to the floor.

He hustled me down the length of the house. As we cut through the kitchen toward the back door, a heavy knock came from the front of the house. Deputy Bobby said a few choice words under his breath, but he didn't slow down. He threw the deadbolt back, opened the door, and shoved me ahead of him out onto the deck. The day still had that perilous half-light, and the hedges, the dune grass, even the ocean all looked cast in lead. The smell of salt water and the stiff breeze helped, though; my head cleared a little, and I felt like I was waking up.

Deputy Bobby was stripping off his disposable gloves. He shoved them into my front pocket, turned me by the shoulders, and said, "Down to the beach, then run. There are stairs that lead back up to the street by the Jeep. Get out of here and go home."

"But—"

"Go!"

He shoved me, and I either had to stumble into a jog or fall flat on my face. I stopped at the steep flight of stairs that led down to the beach, and Deputy

Bobby made a furious gesture. I managed a few of the steps and looked back again. Deputy Bobby was facing the house now, hands out and open at his sides, in a voice meant to carry, he called, "I'm back here. It's just me."

That galvanized me into movement, and I ran.

CHAPTER 7

I wasn't really sure how I made it home. It must have been a fugue state; I remembered bits and pieces of my flight down the stairs—missing steps, catching myself on an old iron rail pitted with rust—and then struggling up the beach, the sand sucking at my steps. I had a vague impression of reaching the Jeep. Of that sense of enervation—as though something vital had been drained out of me, and what had been left behind was marshmallow fluff. And after that, nothing—a big blank until I found myself in the relative darkness of the coach house, still clutching that stupid folder, my face puffy and hot as I listened to the sound of my shallow, rapid breaths in the stillness.

I dragged myself in through the back door. The servants' dining room was warm, and it smelled like freshly baked bread and hot oil and onions that had been cooked just right. I made it to the table, dropped into a seat, and couldn't go any farther.

The sound of my arrival must have been loud enough to reach the kitchen because a moment later, Indira emerged. She was dressed in a wine-colored blouse and patterned trousers, and she looked a hundred percent put together the way she always did, and her witch-white streak of hair stood out like a blaze. Emotions flitted across her face in succession before, in a surprisingly controlled voice, she asked, "Are you all right? What happened?"

I told her.

Indira was silent as she stared at the photos. Then she closed the folder and looked into the middle distance, her expression blank—and terrible in its blankness.

"We went swimming—" I began.

"I know." She pushed the folder toward me. "I thought this might happen."

"You thought this might happen?"

Something in my voice must have roused her because she lifted her eyes to focus on me again. "Not with you, Dash. That's not what I meant. I thought this might happen—to me, actually. Something like this. I'm old enough to know that people are eager to believe the worst. When Keme started spending more time here, I knew it could be a problem. It was a problem, in fact. Vivienne didn't want him around. But then Vivienne left, and you and Keme got along so well—"

I snorted.

A smile lit up Indira's face, and she continued, "And I hoped—well, I didn't even hope. I let myself stop thinking about it."

Now that she reminded me, I remembered how, when I had first come to Hemlock House, she'd been quick to explain the situation with Keme. Because, just like she'd said, I'd been quick to assume the worst.

"I know I shouldn't feel this way, but I'm happy he's dead. Blackmail is an ugly, sordid thing." She hesitated. "Had he contacted you? Did you know what he wanted?"

"That's the weird thing. He did talk to me about buying Hemlock House, but it's not like—I don't know. I mean, it's not like he made a serious offer and I rejected it outright."

Indira made a small sound of acknowledgement. "But he might have been laying the groundwork for it. And if his plan was to force you to sell, probably at significantly less than what the property is worth, then it seems likely he's done this before. You said there were other files."

"I know. I guess that's the next step." I frowned, trying to wrap my head around the investigation. "If this were a mystery novel, you know what would happen? It would all have to do with Halloween. Or it would *look* like it all had to do with Halloween. Like, the wrong person would be killed because they were wearing a costume. Or the killer would switch costumes. Or they'd dress the body up in a costume like *Weekend at Bernie's*. But it's not any of those things. We know who was at that party. And we know plenty of them didn't like him."

"They disliked him enough to kill him?" Indira asked.

"It's hard to say. Maybe. Jen, the woman who runs the surf camp, argued with him about his plans for the camp, and she was seriously angry. You saw Nate Hampton attack him at the beach, and he was skulking around the party." The image of Damian's face floated into view. Reluctantly, I added, "There was a guy there, one of the surfers. I caught a glimpse of him when he was looking at Gerry, and he was definitely feeling…ragey. And those are just the ones I know. There are probably more—I mean, he didn't seem like a lovable guy."

"Clearly."

"The problem, though, is that the only thing we have is motive. That's the only way to approach this. Opportunity is out—we already know these people were at the party, and in the chaos after the fight, anybody could have snuck off and followed Gerry. And in terms of means—well, it doesn't take anything special to shove somebody off a cliff."

"Which leaves the blackmail," Indira said in a thoughtful voice.

"Until we get something more solid. What I'd really like is a connection— something that puts someone out on that cliff with Gerry. Since I don't think we're going to get that, I'd settle for a lie. A nice, big whopper that tells me someone has something to hide." I scratched one eyebrow. "This would be a pain in the patoot to write, you know. Unless you conveniently dropped some evidence later in the book, you'd basically have to engineer a confession."

Indira nodded, but that thoughtful look hadn't left her face. In that same thoughtful voice, she asked, "Dash, are you sure it'll be all right? With you and Keme, I mean."

I nodded. "Since Gerry's dead, I don't think we have much to worry about. It still—well, it freaked me out, I guess. That's every gay guy's nightmare." I tried to inject some good humor into my voice as I added, "The truancy, on the other hand, is definitely a problem. Keme's not going to graduate if he keeps this up."

Some of the strain in her face eased. "You try talking to him about it. I say one word, and he bites my head off. He disappeared for two days last time, and it's getting too cold for him to be sleeping in the timber yard."

There was so much to unpack in that sentence. I was still trying to wrap my head around the fact that Keme not only could talk, but that he did talk—apparently, at length—to just about everyone except me. The fact that he slept rough when he wasn't sleeping in the coach house was news to me; one of the first things I'd learned about Keme was that he had a bad home life, but maybe that had been assuming too much. I was starting to think Keme didn't have a home.

"I might say something, actually," I said. "I have the slight advantage that he won't actually scream at me, since he doesn't talk to me in general. And I'd like him to graduate high school, preferably so he can go to college somewhere far, far away from here."

"Good luck," Indira said.

"He might get angry, sure. But someone needs to tell him."

"Better you than me."

"I mean, we're friends. What's he going to do? Beat me up? Silently?"

Indira patted my hand. Somehow, that made it so much worse.

"Maybe Deputy Bobby can tell him," I said. "Maybe he can say it, and then he can get in his car and drive away. Although then Keme might run after him and hang onto the car, Terminator style. Of course, that won't work because Deputy Bobby probably won't ever talk to me again."

Indira patted my hand again.

So, of course, I told her what I'd left out before: the fight with Deputy Bobby.

"And he was just such a—such a man about it," I said when I finished. "It makes me want to scream."

Indira looked like she was trying not to smile.

"I know," I said sourly. "I'm aware of the irony."

"I'm sure you are, dear."

"It was totally out of line. And inappropriate. And probably illegal. And he has no right to be snooping into my personal life, or trying to control what I do, or judging me for who I want to date."

"Do you want to date this Damian fellow?"

"I don't know. No, probably not. He seems like he'd want to get high and listen to Jack Johnson and go to parties all the time. It would be horrible."

Indira made a small, polite noise that might have meant anything.

"But you know what? It's nice to have someone be interested in me and not have that person be a murder suspect, or a murder victim, or—or living in their mom's basement and trying to convince me that 'online gamer' is a real job."

"And he looked like quite the stone fox."

I blinked.

"Millie sent me a picture," Indira said.

"What kind of life am I living? How did I end up in this micro-dystopia? Don't answer that."

"Are you going to text him? He might not be boyfriend material, but sometimes, Dash, I think you're lonely. And it can be nice to feel appreciated."

"I don't know. I mean, it is kind of—it was for sexual assault, you know? The arrest. Maybe that's not fair to him, but it does kind of worry me."

Indira made that same small noise again.

"Oh no," I said. "No way. Deputy Bobby was still way out of line."

"I didn't say he wasn't."

I stared at her. There was nothing I could read on her face. "Why couldn't he have, you know, pretended to ask for permission first? Or he could have lied. He could have told me it came up when they were investigating Gerry's death."

"Because Bobby isn't a liar."

In the distance, waves broke against the sea cliffs.

"He knew what he was doing," I finally said. "And he knew it was wrong."

With a nod, Indira sat forward and said, "That should tell you something about Bobby. Let me ask you a question: would you be this angry if it had been someone else?"

"What?"

"If someone else had brought you this information. If Millie had known Damian's reputation because, as usual, Millie knew everything about this town. Or if Fox had figured it out—probably from rewatching another season of *Law & Order*. Or if I'd recognized him from somewhere else. Or if Keme had known because all the surfers talked about him."

It took me too long to say, "But it wasn't any of those things. And Deputy Bobby didn't just know. He had to go looking for it. Because he thinks I can't take care of myself. Because he thinks I've got terrible judgment in men. Because he thinks I need—I need to be fixed or taken care of or something. And I don't need that. I certainly don't need that from him, not when he can't even handle his own—"

I managed to stop myself. A flush made me pull at my jacket, and sweat prickled under my arms.

"Do you really believe Bobby thinks those things about you?" Indira asked.

I didn't answer.

"I won't pretend I know what he thinks," Indira said, "or that I know everything that's been said between you two. It's possible he's told you something, or expressed in some way I haven't seen, that he thinks those things.

But from what I *have* seen, I can tell you that you are one of the most important people in Bobby's life."

"That's ridiculous—"

"Dashiell." The vexation in Indira's voice, more than the use of my full name, cut through my hazy thoughts. She continued, "He comes over almost every day. Before his shifts start. Or after. On the weekends, you go on walks together—"

"Hikes," I said.

"They're only hikes if you actually go uphill," she said with unnecessary, um, factitude. "You go out to eat together. Good Lord, last week, you dragged that poor young man to the outlet mall with you. How many times have I walked in on you reading a book, and Bobby's lying on the floor listening to music, or you're watching a show together, or he's being admirably patient while you and Keme play those ridiculous games."

Yes, I thought. Okay. True. "But he's only over here when West is working, and West doesn't like going hiking, and he needed new earbuds and they have a store at the outlet mall—" I stopped, my throat thick. "I mean, I've only known him for a few months."

But that didn't sound true, not when I said it out loud. Because it felt like I'd known Deputy Bobby for a long time. It felt like I'd known him forever. I texted him every day. Heck, as Indira had so ungraciously pointed out, I saw him almost every day. Everything about our friendship had happened so easily, so organically, that I'd never really stopped to think about it.

"He has friends," I said, my voice a little too tight to sound natural. "He has West."

"You should know better than anyone," Indira said, "that it's possible to have a life full of people and still be desperately lonely."

I couldn't look at her, so I looked at the table. Everything blurred and doubled in my vision.

When Indira spoke again, her voice was full of unexpected compassion. "I think that when you said those things to Bobby, you might not have said them because you believe he thinks them. I think, maybe, that Bobby touched a nerve without meaning to." She was silent for a long time. "Do you understand what I'm saying?"

I nodded. "If he was—" So many words presented themselves to me. I chose the only safe one. "—worried about me, why didn't he just tell me?"

The vexation was back in her voice as she said, "I believe you were complaining earlier about someone acting like a man." She rose. "You might consider that he was trying to tell you, Dash, the only way he knew how. You might consider that this is hard for him, and he's doing his best."

I opened my mouth, but nothing came out. Because I didn't know what to say. Because I didn't want to think too much about what Indira was saying. About what she might be saying. Because it was all conjecture, assumptions, based on wildly inaccurate interpretations of, well, everything.

But when I looked up, Indira was staring back at me: those dark, knowing eyes, and that witch's shock of white hair.

A knock came at the door. It had an unfamiliar cadence—labored, almost struggling. But it was strange how you could know a person. All the ways you could know them. The way they looked when they were trying not to laugh at you. (Because, for example, you'd fallen off your bike trying to do a trick you remembered from fifth grade.) The way a room felt when they were in it—how you could know, without even looking, that they were lying on the floor, earbuds in, listening to some band you'd never heard of. Their breathing, maybe. That hint of a clean, masculine smell. Heck, maybe it was their body's electromagnetic field. The way they knocked on the door, and no matter where you were in the house, that sound sent something through you: like someone had plucked a string, and a single, perfect note ran through your body.

"I wonder," Indira said, and her smile was kind because she was always kind, "who that could be?"

CHAPTER 8

The porch light rendered a chiaroscuro Deputy Bobby: the light gleaming on his hair, his eyes, along his jaw, where a hint of very un-Deputy Bobby stubble showed. The rest of him was shadows, just a suggestion of the hollow of his throat, slumped shoulders, the outline of those strong arms. His mouth did something strange, and I realized he was trying to smile.

My conversation with Indira flooded back to me: what she'd said about him; what she'd said about me. My mind went blank, and all I could come up with was "Oh. Hi."

"Hi." It seemed like maybe that was all he could come up with as well, but then, the words labored, he managed, "I wanted to make sure you were okay."

"Yeah. Yeah, I'm fine. God, are you okay?"

His nod was a ghosting movement in the dark. He wasn't standing all that close, but his presence—his silence—was unbearably intimate. I thought this was the Deputy Bobby that maybe nobody else was allowed to see. And I thought, again, about what Indira said. About what it might mean.

Assumptions, I told myself. Interpretations. The reality—cold, hard reality like a sober morning—rushed through me. We were friends. That was all. We'd always be friends.

"I'm sorry about earlier," I said.

He stood there. Behind him, the brittle outlines of hemlocks stirred in the breeze.

"About how I reacted. When you told me. Uh, that stuff about Damian. And yes, I promise I can speak in full sentences, it's just, uh—" I tapped the side of my head. "—a little choppy in here right now."

His breathing was uneven. Like he'd been running, a part of my brain thought. Like he'd run all the way here.

"I know you did it because you want me to be safe," I said. "I know you did it because you're my friend. And I appreciate it, I do. I shouldn't have said what I did. I might be kind of sensitive about dating and relationships and my generally bad judgment in men, but I shouldn't have projected that onto you."

"You don't have to be okay," he said.

"No, I overreacted."

"You can get angry. You can—you can yell."

There was something so strange about his voice, like he wasn't really talking to me, that my reply came out cautiously: "I don't want to yell at you."

"I'm just saying, if you're not okay, that's okay."

"It's okay not to be okay?" I wanted it to sound like a joke, but it fell flat.

Deputy Bobby nodded again, just that suggestion of movement in the darkness. "You can tell me if you're not okay. You can talk to me about it."

"Bobby—" I struggled for a moment, and once again, I came up with a moment of sheer poetic genius: "I'm *fine*."

He did this little breath thing that was so awful I didn't realize, until an instant too late, it had been a laugh. And then, in that way as though he were talking to someone else, he said, "I just wanted to check on you."

"Okay," I said drawing out the word until it was almost a question. But he didn't reply, and he didn't move. "Do you want to come in?"

He shook his head.

I want to take full ownership of this moment and acknowledge that I am not a particularly bright man, because it didn't occur to me until exactly that moment what was happening.

Then I said, "Bobby, are you okay?"

He jerked out a nod.

"Are you sure? Because you don't seem like you're okay. And someone very wise and much, much older than me once told me it was okay not to be okay."

"I, uh—" The way he stopped broke my heart, but it was worse when he tried to smile again. He sounded like he was setting up a joke when he said, "The guys took me in. I had to call West from the station."

"Oh God—"

"It's fine. They didn't arrest me." The pause that came after had a numb quality. "But West told me not to come home tonight."

I waited, but no punchline came. Where the ambient light caught his eyes, his gaze was blank and unprocessing.

"Oh God," I said. "Bobby, I'm so sorry."

"He's really mad."

"It's going to be okay. Come inside."

He didn't move, so I took his arm and brought him into the vestibule. I hadn't bothered with the lights, so we stood together in the shadows. A part of me was aware that I was still holding his arm: solid, dense with muscle. A part of me was aware of the heat of him. And a part of me was aware that he was trembling.

Deputy Bobby put his free hand to his forehead and held it there like he had a headache. "He's so mad."

"I'm sorry, Bobby."

He shook his head, barely more than an impression in the gloom.

"He'll get over it," I said. "It'll all work out."

"He's right to be angry. He should be angry." The only reason I knew he closed his eyes was because that hint of reflected light was extinguished. Despair tilted his voice as he said, "Oh my God."

I should have known better. After that conversation with Indira, I definitely should have known better. But it didn't matter; he was in pain, and he was my friend, and his heartbreak was so intense it felt radioactive. I slipped my arms around him and pulled him against me.

His body was stiff at first, his muscles tense, joints locked into stiff angles. I always forgot I was taller, and it was disorienting how he fit with me, his head resting on my shoulder, his face turned into my neck. His breath was hot on the sensitive skin there. With every breath, I could smell his hair.

The thing you don't learn writing mystery novels? Romance. When Will Gower was a rough-and-ready private eye, he had sex—lots of sex. (Too much sex, if you asked Phil, my parents' agent.) And when he was a jaded cop with a drinking problem, he had sex. And when he was an icily intellectual FBI profiler, he had sex (in one manuscript that will never see the light of day, with the serial killer he was trying to profile). Will Gower got his heart broken by the systemic cruelties of a corrupt world. Will Gower, the white knight who never knew when to give up, lost people he cared about. But he didn't fall in love. And the part of my brain that never turned off, the part of my brain that turned everything into stories, the part of me that recorded details and saved them for the next time I needed them, thought: the way I'm holding him, his shirt is slightly rucked up, and I can feel a hint of bare skin low on his back; the way his hair tickles my nose and I want to sneeze; how he splays his fingers against my ribs, like he's not sure if he's pushing me away or grabbing on. My heart, I thought, like I'd come apart from my body. How fast my heart is beating. And I wanted to turn it into a story, to make it safe and manageable, sewn up from beginning to end. But I didn't know how, and even if I had, I wasn't sure I could bring myself to do it. To take this, all of it, and make it...less.

By degrees, his body softened until he felt real again. And my heart slowed down. A little. Like, there wasn't an imminent risk of a cardiac event. He stirred. His fingers flexed against my side and drew back. I relaxed my arms, and he retreated a step. He tried to look at me, but his eyes were fixed on something behind me, and he rubbed his jaw.

"Let's get you something to eat."

He shook his head.

"Let's sit down, then."

He swallowed, and it looked painful. "I should go."

"Bobby," I said.

And now he did look at me. I didn't know exactly what to call what I saw in his face. A plea, maybe. Asking me for—what?

I changed what I'd been about to say. "Where are you going to spend the night?"

"I don't know. The Rock On."

The Rock On Inn was adorable, but I said, "No way. Cheri-Ann will put it on Facebook two minutes after you check in."

Deputy Bobby rubbed his eyes.

"You can stay here," I said.

"No."

"Yes, it's perfect. There's a million bedrooms, and they're all haunted, plus secret passages for easy murdering, and all those taxidermy birds to stare at you while you try to sleep."

He stopped rubbing and just pressed his fingers against his eyes. "Dash, I can't—"

"You can. It'll be fine. Do you—I mean, did you have, like, a bag or something?"

He nodded.

"I'll grab it," I said. "Be right back."

"No, I can—"

I squeezed past him and jogged out into the night.

The air was cool verging on cold, with a snap to it, and after the relative warmth of the house, my glasses fogged. Or maybe that was my breath, because it certainly felt like I was overheated, like I was drawing in lungfuls of the mist as I tried to bring my body temperature down. I wiped my hands on my jeans when I got to his Pilot, and as I opened the door, I thought, What am I doing?

Before I could consider that question more carefully, I grabbed the backpack from the passenger seat and hurried back inside.

Deputy Bobby was standing where I'd left him, a silhouette in the murky vestibule.

"Sure you don't want anything to eat?" I asked.

He didn't respond.

"Come on," I said.

I had to touch his arm to get him moving, but after that, I was careful to keep my hands to myself. We moved through the house in the dark, heading for the central staircase. I kept to the rugs. I went slowly on the stairs. The sounds of our steps were muffled, but they seemed magnified in the house's silence. I felt like I'd gone back in time, like I was sixteen and sneaking Justin Anderson into my bedroom to make out. In the thick shadows, every shape became Indira, and a flash fire went through my face. Not because she would think badly of me. Not because she would even care. But because of what she'd said earlier. Because a part of me was still running away from that conversation.

And look, a part of my brain pointed out, how well that's going.

I led Deputy Bobby down the hall and into one of Hemlock House's many bedrooms. The house was so quiet that I could hear every noise: the rattle of the door's old hardware, the ancient latch squeaking back, Deputy Bobby's ragged breathing. The bedroom itself looked like all the others in Hemlock House: the damask wallpaper, the four-poster bed, the cavernous fireplace, a gilt candelabra that looked like something straight out of Castle Dracula (perfect for holding dramatically while standing on a staircase). The mirror above the dressing table caught us, and for a strange moment, everything was reversed.

Shaking off the sensation, I carried Deputy Bobby's bag to the bed. He trailed after me into the room, his steps soft and scuffing. "Welcome to Dashiell Dawson Dane's bed-and-breakfast. Bathroom is through there—it's a Jack-and-Jill, so we share it, which means remember to lock the door. We have some very important house rules, so I'm going to ask you to pay attention. First, we have a strict policy about not getting out of bed before noon. We put the bed in bed-and-breakfast."

Apparently, even in the depths of despair, Deputy Bobby could still roll his eyes.

"Second, breakfast is whatever Indira is gracious enough to make. And if she decides not to make anything, we're going to Chipper, and you're buying me the Dash Special."

"It's not really a special, you know." His voice sounded like he was fighting for normal. "And I don't see why you have to have all four breakfast sandwiches at the same time."

"Wait, someone told you about the Dash Special?"

"Millie put it on the menu board."

"Oh my God." I drew a deep breath. "Third, if you're going to search for hidden treasure, please don't break anything."

"What was it this time?"

"Keme tried to climb a downspout."

Deputy Bobby rubbed his eyes, but he looked like he was trying not to smile.

"And fourth, if you need anything—anything—please tell me." I put my hands on my hips and said in my sternest voice, "Please."

He nodded.

"I'll get out of your hair," I said.

He nodded. Whatever animation had filled his face was draining away again, and he looked around the room as though still trying to take it in, his expression dull.

"Or," I said, "I could stay."

I got another nod.

There aren't a lot of times in my life I've been brave, but I think maybe this one counted. Black spots flecked my vision. It felt like somebody else was breathing through my mouth. My guts had collapsed into that black hole of whirling, sharp objects. But somehow, I managed to say, "Bobby?"

He looked at me.

"I'm going to stay. Just until I'm sure you're okay."

Nothing. But I saw in his eyes—what? That plea again, maybe, although I didn't know what he was asking for. A hint of panic. He began to pace, moving his way back and forth across the room. I sank onto a chaise. Springs compressed under me, groaning. The scrolled wood of the back felt cold, and my hand was slick and oily. Deputy Bobby moved from the dressing table and the backwards world inside the mirror to the fireplace. He studied the porcelain figure of a woman there. He touched the tortoiseshell lid of a trinket box. He had broad shoulders and a narrow waist, and even now, the vee of his body was strong and straight.

"What's going on with your parents?" he asked as he moved to study a massive oil painting of a—I want to say a stallion. (And again, I have to emphasize in Millie style: MASSIVE.)

"What's going on with them?" I asked. "I don't know. I guess the usual. They don't talk to each other. Then they talk about writing. Dad cleans his guns. Or he shoots his guns. Or he goes down to the gunsmith and talks to the guys and buys a new gun. Mom reads court transcripts or books about psychopaths or medical journals. She gets the eggs from the chickens. She checks herself into a residential treatment program."

Deputy Bobby jerked his gaze toward me.

"She's fine," I said. "She does it almost every year. She thinks she's going to get some dramatic inside scoop, you know? Like, uncover abuse, or meet someone who will inspire a character. That kind of thing."

"Does it work?"

"God, no. The places she picks are practically spas."

Deputy Bobby laughed, but it faded quickly. "I meant what about your story?"

"What?"

"Your story. For the anthology."

"You already asked me about that."

"I know."

"It's been, I don't know, a couple of hours. It's not like I drove home after almost being caught by the police and suddenly had the muse whispering in my ear."

"I meant—" He turned away again, tracing the back of a slipper chair with one hand. "Like, what do your parents say?"

Talking about my writing always opened that black hole in my stomach, and talking about my parents and my writing was like turning those spinning blades up to ten. But I'd worked hard on not reacting to those feelings. And this was, after all, Deputy Bobby. I took a deep breath. And then another. I watched him: the way his hand followed the back of the chair, the way he angled his body away from me, the slight hunch to his shoulders. And because I'm so very, very smart, it only took me that long to realize, once again, we weren't really talking about me.

"Well, they haven't said anything yet. And I really am going to try to finish that story. But I won't. I mean, I probably won't. And my dad will get angry and give me this gruff, manly speech about 'digging down deep' and 'doing the work.' And my mom will have a panic attack, and once that's over, she'll spend six weeks researching every therapist in a hundred miles and start making appointments for me."

The look on Deputy Bobby's face was priceless.

"This is why I always tell people it's a good thing that they forget about me most of the time." I kept my gaze on his face as I asked, "What about your parents?"

He shook his head, and his hand stilled on the back of the chair. "They're good people."

I thought I could hear the clock ticking in the hall. After what might have been a minute, I said, "They must be excited that you and West are going to move back to Portland."

"I guess." Deputy Bobby gave a pained laugh. "My mom is. I mean, she loves West. Loves him. My family jokes that she loves him more than she loves me. My dad—who knows? I told you about the apartment thing, right?"

I nodded.

"It's like that. Actually, that's good, to be honest. A lot of time, it's nothing. We don't say anything. West and I go back to visit, and he'll say, 'How long are you going to be here?' And that's it. That's the only thing we'll hear all weekend. The first time I took West to meet them, West tried so hard. He kept asking questions. He was so polite. And my mom answered all the questions, no matter how hard West tried to get my dad to talk. He thought my dad was mad at him until I told him that's how it always is."

When I realized he wasn't going to say anything else, I said, "That sounds hard."

"It's...it is what it is." He shook his head. "God, if West breaks up with me, they're going to be furious."

"West isn't going to break up with you."

"It was bad enough in college when I told them I was gay. And they lost their minds when I told them that I wasn't going to med school and, instead, I was going into law enforcement—and, on top of that, I was moving across the state." His mouth twisted. "My mom lost her mind. My dad went out to the garage and didn't come back inside until I left. If West breaks up with me, that's strike three."

It was such a strange thing to say that I didn't know how to respond. The wind batted at the panes in the old windows, swallowing the tick of the clock.

"I just don't know what to do," Deputy Bobby burst out. "I don't know what to say. I don't know how to—I don't know how to talk to him about it. My parents never fight. They never disagree. They never talk. But everything I do lately seems to make West angry. More than angry. And I want to say something, I want to talk to him, I want to fix it. It's my fault. I know I can fix it." His knuckles blanched as he gripped the back of the chair. "But I open my mouth, and it's like—remember what you said about razor blades? It's like that. I can't think. I can't talk. I can't get a single word out of my mouth. I just freeze." That unhappy laugh boiled up again. "But I'm talking to you, so what's the matter with me?"

"Nothing's the matter with you. Talking to me isn't the same as talking to West. With West, there's more on the line. That's a lot of pressure. It can be scary."

"I do fine with pressure. I'm under pressure all day."

"I know. I just mean there's more at stake. He's so important to you."

Deputy Bobby shook his head, but his hand relaxed around the back of the chair.

"You could try writing it down," I said. "I could help you. You could write down everything you want to say to him, and then when you're ready to talk, you've got it right there. You'll look like a total dingus, but you always look like a total dingus, so West won't even notice."

His laugh was sudden and shocked. But it was also real. And for the first time in what felt like an eternity, he flashed that goofy smile at me.

"This is why we're friends," I said. "I have all the best ideas."

"It's a terrible idea."

"It's an amazing idea. I literally solved all your problems in like fifteen seconds."

"You didn't solve all my problems. You are like eighty percent of my problems."

"Only eighty? I need to try harder."

I got that goofy grin again.

"Well?" I asked.

It felt like a long time before he said, "Maybe." And then, more quietly, "Thank you."

"How about we make a deal?"

"Dash, I can't eat an entire birthday cake by myself. I definitely don't want to eat one by myself."

"No, that was a challenge, and only because Keme—it doesn't matter. How about this? I'll finish my story. Even though it's going to mean pulling my hair out, and ripping out my fingernails, and screaming into the void as I face my total lack of talent—"

"You've been spending too much time with Fox."

"—and you write down what you want to say to West and have a conversation with him. Explain what's going on. He loves you. You love him. You need to work this out. Plus it makes me super sad when you're sad. And I don't want to be sad. I want to be happy. And full of cake. Like, an entire cake, even though Keme doesn't think I could do it."

He came across the room to where I sat on the chaise, and he looked down at me. The dark bronze of his eyes looked even darker than usual because his pupils were swollen, and the angle, with me staring up at him, made it hard to read his expression. He was close enough I could feel him again, that awareness of his body like a sixth sense making the hairs on my arms stand up.

"I'm sorry," he said. It was like a spell breaking. I was suddenly aware of my flushed cheeks, the heat under my breastbone, the tingling hollowness of my legs. "About earlier."

I stared at him, unable to bring out any words.

"Damian," he said.

"Oh."

"You were right. I was out of line."

I shook my head because I didn't trust my voice.

He crouched. He put his hands on my knees. To steady himself, maybe. Or maybe not. They felt like anchors, and the rest of me was trying to float away. He looked me in the eye and said, "You are a good friend. I want you to be happy too."

I listened to the rhythm of our breaths. Felt the warm weight of his hands. For an instant, he seemed to have his own gravity, and I felt myself tumbling toward him, tipping into him.

And then he adjusted his weight, moving back a fraction, steadying himself, a hint of a self-conscious smile, like a boy wobbling while he tried to do a trick. And it was over.

CHAPTER 9

Big surprise: I didn't sleep at all.

I should have been exhausted. I *was* exhausted. Emotionally, intellectually, physically. After making sure Deputy Bobby was settled, I went to my room and collapsed.

Instead of sleep, though, I lay there, staring up at the canopy, replaying every word of the conversation, every pause, every movement, every angle. I'd been so encouraging. I'd been so supportive. I groaned and dragged a pillow over my face. I'd offered to help him fix things with West.

At excruciating length, I considered one important question: what in the world was wrong with me?

Around three in the morning, though, I stopped worrying about that question because I remembered something else.

I had promised to finish that stupid story.

Why, I wanted to know. Why had I said that? Because it had seemed…right at the time. Because it had seemed like a show of solidarity. Because, if I peered uncomfortably into the deeper waters of my soul, it had been something I could offer him. And, of course, because it had been Deputy Bobby.

I wailed (silently). I gnashed my teeth (careful not to chip the enamel). I got out of bed. I got back into bed. I grabbed my laptop. I put my laptop back.

I decided now was the perfect time to give the bathroom a quick scrub—after all, I wanted it to be clean for Deputy Bobby.

I had scoured three quarters of the tub when I reached the tipping point. I washed my hands, sprinted to the laptop, and started typing as fast as I could. And, an hour and a half later (not counting the two breaks I took to indulge in sweaty panic attacks), I was done. It wasn't a long story, and I'd already drafted most of it at various stages. And because it was a short story, the premise was simple: Will Gower, a private investigator on the mean streets of Portland, Oregon, was hired to investigate the disappearance of a missing man. The only clue? An unsigned letter asking the missing man to meet at a place known only as "the eagle's nest." Because Will Gower knows the underbelly of the city like nobody else, he recognizes the reference: a local crime lord names all his safe houses after different birds. Will Gower rushes off, and of course, he's dead wrong. (A poor choice of words, maybe—I mean, I can't kill Will Gower.)

It's one of the oldest tricks in the mystery writer's handbook. A piece of evidence appears to mean one thing, but it actually means something else. The deftest handling of this leads the reader to make their own misinterpretation (Christie is the master of this, of course). But even someone ham-handed like me can make it work if the protagonist knows—or thinks he knows—what the clue might mean.

(Spoiler alert: The Eagle's Nest is also, it turns out, the name of a café that closed years ago—and had once been where our missing man used to meet with his lover. Once Will Gower figures out this second meaning to the clue, the rest of the story falls into place, and the jilted lover confesses to murder. See? Easy peasy.)

It might not have been a great story. It might not have even been a good story. But it had—energy, I guess. If you've ever picked up something and known, from the first page, that there was *something* there, even if you didn't know exactly what, it felt like that. The voice was part of it; I knew Will Gower's voice, and I knew what those dark, rain-washed streets would be like. And I liked the twist. The plot might need a little more development, maybe one more complication—

Before I could go too far down that road, I said a hundred Hail Marys (I didn't say any—I wouldn't even know how to start) and I emailed my dad the file.

The wave hit me all at once:

Everyone was going to hate it.

It was garbage.

He was going to be so disappointed.

But there wasn't any way to unsend the email, and so, after wallowing for a while, I dragged myself to the bathroom. I finished cleaning, and then I showered and got dressed. I hadn't heard any movement from Deputy Bobby's room. Maybe he'd taken me seriously about the *we put the bed in bed-and-breakfast* thing. More likely, he was even more exhausted than I was.

Indira wasn't in the kitchen or the servants' dining room, but she'd left huckleberry pancakes, and I found my stash of emergency syrup. (There's a secret compartment, no joke, in the floor of the butler's pantry. Intended, no doubt, for people like me, who were the unjustly targeted victims of Keme and Indira's campaign to, quote, "not eat like you're in the movie *Elf*.")

The pancakes were still warm, by the way. That's real love.

As I ate, my mind turned to Gerry's murder. I was convinced now that it had been murder. And I suspected the murder had something to do with the blackmail Gerry had kept in his safe. I took out my phone and swiped through the photos I'd taken during those last, frantic minutes of my search with Deputy Bobby. So many names I didn't recognize. Financial paperwork. Photos of, uh, compromising situations. Gerry had been a class act. And as I swiped, I found myself turning over, in the back of my head, what Jen had told us: Gerry's interest in younger men. That was fine, of course, unless it became predatory. And judging by the way Gerry had pretty much groped me in public, I didn't think Gerry was the take-no-for-an-answer type.

I was so caught up in that train of thought that I almost missed a name I *did* recognize. I swiped back, zoomed in, and stared. The file was for Nate Hampton: used-car salesman and city councilor for Hastings Rock. The same man, conveniently enough, who had attacked Gerry at the surfing competition.

It took me a few minutes of zooming in and reading the documents I'd taken pictures of to realize what I was seeing. One of the documents showed a statement for an account titled "Hastings Rock Sewage Improvement Fund." And the second document was a statement for Nathan R. Hampton's personal checking account. You didn't have to be a financial genius to see the money moving into the Sewage Improvement Fund and then being transferred to Nate's private account. Nate Hampton, who was on the city council. Nate Hampton, who had attacked Gerry at the surfing competition.

I sat, listening to the house's silence. Still nothing from Deputy Bobby. It was an ungodly hour (nine o'clock), and I didn't want to risk waking him. Plus, I didn't want him to get in trouble with West again for involving himself in the investigation. Besides, I wasn't even sure what I was going to do. Maybe I wouldn't do anything. Maybe I'd just go for a drive and scope things out.

Sure, I thought.

I grabbed my keys and headed to the coach house.

CHAPTER 10

Hampton Automotive was on the outskirts of Hastings Rock, located on a prime patch along the state highway. It looked like any used-car dealership: a big, illuminated sign; an enormous lot filled with cars and crossovers and trucks, and yes, even the occasional minivan; pennants strung overhead, fluttering in the wind. I couldn't find a parking spot, so I wedged the Jeep along a red stretch of curb near the service department's roll-up door. Maybe, I considered, at that exact moment, Deputy Bobby's internal parking monitor was going off. Maybe he was sitting straight up in bed, eyes glowing, his whole body energized with the possibility of writing me one final parking ticket.

But I sincerely hoped not.

When I got out of the Jeep, the sound of the pennants' snapping met me, and from farther off, the boom of hearty, middle-aged-man laughter. It took me a moment to spot the group: a big guy with a goatee not unlike Gerry's, in a sport coat and a striped button-up, thundering more laughter as he guided a young couple toward what appeared to be much more car than they could afford. The day was bright, the sky fringed with puffy clouds to the west, and one of those inflatable tube men wobbled and cast a dancing shadow across the lot. The air was crisp to the point of making my teeth ache, and my first deep breath caught the smell of fresh paint and rubber. I decided I seriously (seriously, this time) needed to dig around and find my winter coats.

Inside, Muzak met me (Taylor Swift crossed with a synthesizer), and the smell of freshly popped popcorn mixed now with the odor of new tires. It was a large, open room, with glass walls on three sides, and amidst the decorative straw bales and plastic pumpkins and a little animatronic witch's head that cackled every time someone walked past it, someone had parked sixty thousand dollars' worth of Audi. A woman in a black dress made her way toward me. I recognized her from the Otter Slide, and I thought her name was Maya.

"Welcome to Hampton Automotive," she said. "How can I help you today?"

I glanced around. "I had an appointment with Mr. Hampton."

"Oh." Maya looked toward the back of the room, where cubicles offered the illusion of privacy. "He's finishing up a sale right now. If you wanted to look at something in particular, Mr. Dane, I can help you until he's free."

Small town. Small, small town. "No, thanks. I'll just putz around until he's free. Maya, right?"

She smiled at me. "Let me know if you need anything."

As Maya returned to her desk, I meandered—purposefully. Without making it too obvious, I let my rambling take me toward the cubicles at the back. I pretended to look at the Audi. I pretended to be impressed with the decorative hay bales. I pretended to have an obscene amount of interest in a poster on the wall explaining Hampton Auto's lifetime alignment policy. I was inching toward a row of chairs, complete with while-you-wait pamphlets on an end table, when Maya's voice broke through the Muzak.

"Hampton Automotive wishes you a happy Halloween," she said. "This season, treat yourself to one of our new arrivals."

I looked around. I was the only one in the showroom.

Maya wore a wry grin as she lowered the phone from her mouth and stage-whispered, "I have to do it every fifteen minutes."

And, by sheer coincidence, at that moment I arrived at the chairs lined up outside Nate's cubicle. I got a glimpse of the space inside: plaques on the walls announcing the DEAL OF THE MONTH, which apparently Nate had a track record of winning (and awarding to himself); framed print advertisements for Hampton Automotive, all of them featuring a close-up of Nate's face; a photo of a billboard (guess whose face?); and, just for giggles, novelty foam car keys as long as a yardstick. Nate sat behind a particleboard desk, nodding enthusiastically as an older couple explained something about their finances; to judge by Nate's face, he was from the wait-for-an-opening-to-talk school of listening. A whiff of overpowering cologne wafted out, and I hurried past the opening and dropped into a seat.

"—can't afford it, Nathan," the woman was saying. "We're on a fixed income. In fact, we shouldn't even be here—"

"Right, Mrs. Carlson," said Nate. "Right. Right. But the way I see it, you can't afford not to buy it. This is the deal of a lifetime. I'm practically giving you this car."

"It's a good deal, Betty," the man said. "The deal of a lifetime."

"Listen to your husband, Mrs. Carlson. You don't want to do something stupid."

It was refreshing, I thought, to have a front-row seat, so to speak, to somebody else sticking his foot in his mouth.

"Excuse me?" Mrs. Carlson said.

"I mean—"

"Listen to me, Nathan Hampton. I swatted your bum in preschool, and you're not too old for me to swat it again."

"No, that's not what I—"

"Roger, we're leaving."

"No, please, Mrs. Carlson—"

"And you'd better believe I'm going to be telling the gardening club about this."

Nate's breathing had a slightly strangled quality to it. "You can't—no, no, wait—"

But Mrs. Carlson—who did, to be fair, look like a bit of a battleaxe—tromped out of the cubicle, with Mr. Carlson (who had a snazzy suede jacket that looked a million years old) close on her heels.

Nate let out a short, deep noise of frustration, and something slammed into the desk. A moment later, he emerged from the cubicle, his face red.

"Maya—" he barked.

"Hi, Nate," I said.

He jumped as though I'd goosed him, but he recovered quickly. After giving me a once-over, he said, "Have we met?"

"Not officially. I saw you at the surfing competition." Standing, I offered my hand. "Dash."

"I know who you are."

"Good. That makes things easier. I was wondering if you'd have a few minutes to talk."

He made an effort, I'll give him that: his face reassembled itself into something approaching politeness, and he even tried out a wooden smile. "Of course. Give me a minute, and I'll be happy to show you around."

"Oh, no. I don't want to buy a car. In fact, I probably shouldn't even be driving at all. More of a bike man, I think. Fewer casualties that way. Plus, the tickets."

"Uh, right."

"I want to talk to you about Gerry Webb's murder."

The flush mottling Nate's face drained away.

In a quieter voice, I said, "Let's sit down. I have some photos I'd like to show you."

Nate shook his head—weakly at first, and then more forcefully. "I don't have to—" He stopped and started again. "You need to leave. Right now."

"That's a bad decision, Nate. A terrible decision. Because if I leave, I'm going to talk to the sheriff, and I really don't think you want me to talk to the sheriff."

He wavered, and I thought I had him. Then he said, "Get out." He pushed past me, snapped something at Maya, and pushed through a fire door; I glimpsed a more utilitarian space beyond, which I guessed was the service garage, and the door swung shut.

Maya was staring at me, so I made my way over to her.

"I am so sorry," she said, "but Mr. Hampton asked me to make sure you leave."

"That's okay," I said. "I don't want to cause you any problems. I just wanted to ask—"

I was about to launch into a few questions about Nate—shots in the dark, mostly, hoping I'd get lucky. But then the door opened, and the salesman in the sports coat and the striped shirt maneuvered the young couple inside. He had his hands on their shoulders, and he was talking so loudly that, even from across the room, my ears were ringing. His volume rose even more, though, as he delivered what sounded like the punchline to a joke: "And the man says, 'You have to keep your worms warm.'" Without missing a beat, he looked over at Maya and me and shouted, "Maya, let's get Robby and Nina something to drink."

The young couple exchanged pained glances, although that might have had more to do with the fact that the salesman had a death grip on their shoulders.

"Excuse me," Maya said.

It all came together in an instant: who Nate Hampton was, and what he wanted—the DEAL OF THE MONTH plaques, his face in every advertisement, the instant groveling when Mrs. Carlson had gotten angry. I wasn't a psychiatrist or a psychologist or a therapist. If you asked Keme, I wasn't even allowed to use the microwave without adult supervision (although that was one time, and I only forgot the spoon because I was so excited about the hot fudge). But you spend enough time writing about people, thinking about people, trying to get inside their heads, and you learn a thing or two. Plus, it doesn't hurt to have a mom who checks herself into psych wards for fun.

I nodded and asked, "Do you mind if I use your phone? My battery is almost dead."

"Oh sure. You press this button to dial out." And then, with an apologetic smile, Maya hurried to get Robby and Nina something to drink. I was guessing they'd like a big helping of cyanide.

I gave the phone's complicated array of buttons a quick study. And then I picked up the receiver and pressed a button. The Muzak overhead cut off, and my voice echoed over the sound system.

"Hi, everyone. My name is Dash, and I'm excited to wish you a happy Halloween from Hampton Automotive. We've got some tricks and some treats for you today. Our first treat is going to be a dramatic reading about Mr. Nate Hampton and the Hastings Rock Sewage Improvement Fund—he loves tricks, and I'm going to share one of his best ones with you."

That was as far as I got before Nate Hampton—who cared about approval and validation and awards and being liked (and who also probably had a healthy interest in not going to prison)—burst into the showroom. The color was high in his cheeks, and his eyes were glassy as he stared around the room. Maya was staring back. Robby and Nina were staring back. The salesman seemed to have forgotten whatever he was saying (probably another joke), and it looked like Nina might try to make a break for it.

I cocked my head at Nate in question.

"Sorry about that, folks," Nate called with a quite frankly unbelievable attempt at good cheer. "Dash loves playing jokes on us. Excuse me for a minute."

I gave my tiny audience a rueful smile and hung up the phone.

"What are you doing?" Nate asked in a furious whisper as he came toward me. "Are you out of your mind?"

"Why don't we talk about that?"

Nate shot another look at the salesman and the hostages—er, customers. "Hurry up," he said and stalked off.

Instead of heading for his cubicle, though, he led me through a door marked EMPLOYEES ONLY. Behind us, excited conversation broke out, but the door swung shut, cutting it off. A short hallway connected with a pair of restrooms, a cramped kitchenette, and what appeared to be storerooms. Above a toaster oven, a poster showed a smiling Nate Hampton and THE ABC'S OF HAMPTON AUTOMOTIVE: ALWAYS BE CLOSING. I caught a whiff of Totino's pizza and despair.

Spinning to face me, Nate asked, "What do you want?"

"I want to talk to you about Gerry Webb's murder."

"I don't know anything about that."

"But you can see why I'd find that hard to believe, right? I saw Gerry's files. I know he was blackmailing you."

Nate flinched. He couldn't quite meet my eyes as he mumbled, "It was a misunderstanding. I didn't—I wouldn't—"

"I don't care about the embezzlement. Well, I do, but I'm not here to talk about that. How much were you paying Gerry?"

"Huh?"

"The blackmail. How much was he taking you for?"

"I wasn't paying him." And then, as though I were a little slow, he said, "He wanted help with the zoning and the permits for his development."

That explained one thing: how Gerry had gotten permission to build on sacred land.

"That's all?" I asked.

"That's all? Man, do you know how hard that was? I busted my hump making it happen. Ruined my reputation in town, too. Half the people around here think I was getting kickbacks from Gerry, and the other half think I'm out of my mind."

"That must be hard," I said. "But once you got him the permits, what did Gerry start squeezing you for?"

"Nothing. I already told you."

"Then why did you attack him at the surfing competition?"

A hint of color rose in Nate's cheeks. "He told me he'd let me invest in the development. After I'd fixed everything, though, he told me he already had a partner, and he wasn't interested in adding someone else. I tried to let it go, but I couldn't stop thinking about it. I just kept thinking and thinking. And then I saw him at that stupid competition, and—I didn't even know what I was doing. It was like somebody else was doing it, you know?"

I wasn't sure I believed all of that, but I believed part of it. Somebody as desperate for validation as Nate would have to work himself up to that level of aggression; it would take a lot to force him out of the patterns of placating and pleading I'd seen from him today. The real question, though, was what had happened after the surf challenge. Had that attack at the beach been an isolated incident? Or had Nate whipped himself into a frenzy again after his public humiliation?

"How long has Gerry been blackmailing you?"

"I don't know. A year. A little more. He showed up here one day. He introduced himself, told me he had an eye on some land, wanted to talk to me about a business opportunity. I told him no way—getting on the bad side of the Confederated Tribes is a sure way to piss off pretty much everybody in town. I thought that was the end of it. The next time I saw him, he was at my front door showing me—"

"Showing you what?"

"You know. Papers."

I nodded. "Where were you during the Halloween party?"

"I don't know, man. I had some drinks. Moved around. I wasn't exactly invited."

"That's the best you can do?"

"What do you want me to say? I was right there."

A question struck me. "Why were you there?"

Nate grimaced. "One of the surfers. She and I—I mean, it's a small town. And when it's not tourist season, we don't get a lot of new faces."

"Any chance she can tell me where you were?"

"No." He sounded even more miserable than when he'd been confessing. "She said she didn't like gingers." Then his gaze came toward me, and his voice sharpened, "You know who you should be talking to? That protester. The crazy one."

He meant Ali Rivas, I was pretty sure. I asked, "Why's that?"

"Because she's crazy! She'll do anything. She breaks into the construction site. She smashes the windows, and they have to replace them. She puts sugar in the gas tanks of the heavy equipment. She was costing Gerry a fortune, you know? They hated each other."

"She wasn't at the party that night."

"Man, she goes wherever she wants, whenever she wants. Hey, wait! She *was* there—I heard about it. She broke the windows at the surf camp that night."

Now that he said it, I did remember something about broken windows from my visit to the surf camp the next day—my chat with Damian, Jen's anger, the clean-up effort.

"And that's not all," Nate said, excitement making him speak faster. "Gerry had something on her. He got something. Like he did, you know, with me. I heard him talking about her at the party. About how she wasn't going to be a problem any longer."

"That's kind of a convenient thing to remember when you're the prime candidate for a murder."

"I'm telling you the truth. I heard him say it, and I remember feeling sorry for her—once Gerry set his sights on somebody, he'd find something to use against them."

He certainly had with me, although I wasn't going to share that with Nate. "There's kind of a problem with that, though. Aside from how it's a little too neat. I saw Gerry's files, remember? And he didn't have anything on Ali Rivas."

The look Nate gave me verged on pitying. "Yeah, man. Duh. Whoever killed him took their file."

CHAPTER 11

Here's the good news: I didn't get a ticket for parking next to the service garage.

As I drove away from Hampton Automotive, though, I wasn't happy. I considered what Nate had said. I should have considered the possibility that whoever had killed Gerry had managed to access the safe and remove anything incriminating. After all, it had been easy for me and Bobby to get into the safe—the key had been right there. But if the file had been taken, then anybody could be Gerry's killer.

I knew two things, though. First, I didn't trust Nate. I needed to try to verify his alibi (if you could call it that) for the time when Gerry was killed, but I didn't have high hopes. And second, although I wasn't sure I believed Nate's story, I needed to talk to Ali Rivas. Even if the blackmail story wasn't true, she had her own reasons to want Gerry Webb to disappear, and I was curious to hear her side of things.

The problem, though, was that I wasn't really any further in the investigation. I had added a new suspect—Ali had been at the party, and she had her own reasons for wanting to get rid of Gerry. And I wanted to know how Ali kept getting into the camp, in spite of all that security. Did she have help? Was someone hoping that the vandalism would eventually make Gerry—what? Sell? Give up his share of the camp?

Adding a suspect, though, had only made the investigation more complicated. I had too many suspects. And too many motives. And not enough of anything else. What I needed was physical evidence, something irrefutable to tie the killer to Gerry's murder. And, barring that, what I needed was something to maneuver the killer into confessing. The ideal thing to do (if this were a mystery novel) would be to manipulate the killer by claiming to have found a backup copy of the blackmail. The killer would then expose themselves by trying to recover it. But if Nate was correct, and if the killer had already recovered and destroyed their blackmail file from Gerry's safe, then they might be feeling safe and secure. It would take more than an unsubstantiated claim to lure them out of hiding.

Unfortunately, I didn't *have* anything, and nothing presented itself as I drove back to Hemlock House. I called Deputy Bobby on the way; I wanted to tell him—and the Last Picks—what I'd learned. Somebody might know more about Nate. Or about Ali. Or about something I hadn't considered. Maybe Millie's network of town gossip had picked up the perfect clue, and all I had to do was ask. Deputy Bobby didn't answer, so I left him a message telling him I needed to talk. I tried one more time, but I got voicemail again, so I focused on driving.

My route took me south along the state highway. I passed through Hastings Rock. On a day like today, with the sky an intense, vast blue and the sun casting cut-glass shadows, the town looked like what it was supposed to be: a postcard destination, a perfect hodgepodge of dollhouse buildings rising from the bay to the bluffs. The oaks and maples were starting to turn, and scattered with the deep green of pine and spruce were flashes of gold and copper and red.

I was leaving town on the south side when I noticed the Jeep was handling differently. A little stiff. A little less responsive. I started up a small hill, and the engine seemed to hesitate, even when I fed it more gas. As I crested the hill and reached the tunnel of the spruce forest, I passed from the brilliance of a seaside day into the perpetual shadow under the canopy. That was when I noticed that the Jeep's dash lights were flickering. A red warning light popped on—the battery.

At the exact same time, the Jeep shuddered. The steering wheel stiffened as the power steering went out. The hiss of air in the vents went silent. The Jeep gave another of those shudders, and it startled me out of my daze. I wrenched the wheel to the right, trying to wrestle it to the shoulder. The engine sputtered, the Jeep hitched, and then, with a final lurch, it died.

I had enough presence of mind to shift into neutral, and the last of the Jeep's momentum was enough to let us trundle off the state highway and onto the side of the road. Adrenaline coursed through me too late: even though my brain knew I was safe now, my body couldn't slow down the flood of hormones. My hands started to shake. My mouth tasted sour. I felt lightheaded, and I gripped the steering wheel to keep myself upright and steady.

After a few deep breaths, I felt a little better. I forced the shifter into park, set the emergency brake, and took out my phone. It hadn't been that bad, I told myself. It had been the surprise more than anything. I was safe. I was fine. It was a quiet stretch of road, and I was lucky there hadn't been any other cars around when it happened. When I glanced at my phone, though, I felt a little less lucky—like lots of spots up and down the coast, this was apparently a dead zone. Which meant I could either walk back to town, walk to Hemlock House, or wait and hope someone would stop.

Before I had to make a decision, movement in the rearview mirror caught my eye. A car came over the hill—a dark sedan. The driver must have seen me because they slowed and eased onto the side of the road. They must have been extra cautious because they stopped a long way back.

I opened the door and got out of the Jeep. Down the road, the driver was getting out of their car. I squinted, trying to make out details through the thick shade and the distance. Dark pants. Dark shirt. Dark...mask?

No, my brain said automatically. That couldn't be right.

But it was. The driver was wearing a balaclava.

In October.

In Oregon.

On a beautifully bright, sunny day.

A fresh wave of adrenaline began to pump through me. That sick-sour churn of my stomach started again. My vision felt funny—off, somehow. Because, a detached voice inside me said, your eyes are dilating in response to the hormones. Not that I could process the words. I couldn't think about anything. All I could hear was a drumbeat getting faster and faster inside my head.

The masked figure started up the shoulder toward me. They were carrying something in their hand—something small, something made of metal.

My rational brain gave one final protest. This was impossible. It was the middle of the day. It was a state highway. There would be cars, there would be people, there would be witnesses.

Which sounded all well and good and logical. Except where the heck was everybody?

The masked figure had closed a quarter of the distance. They weren't running. They must have realized they didn't need to run. I was just standing there. Staring. Like a moron.

I considered my options: lock myself in the Jeep, or run. The Jeep wasn't a bad bet unless they had a gun. But they probably did have a gun. So, I ran.

The ground sloped down from the shoulder of the road, falling sharply into a wooded ravine. I pushed through a line of ferns, slipped on wet leaf litter, and almost went rolling the rest of the way down. Somehow, I recovered and caught my balance. A shout made me glance back. The masked figure was running toward me now. Behind them, another vehicle had finally appeared—a dark SUV barreling along the state highway. Too little, too late, I thought, and I hurried as best I could down the hill.

If you've never run down a wet, slippery hill before while a masked figure chases you, let me tell you: it's not as easy (or as fun) as it sounds. Every step threatened to send my feet sliding out from under me. The soil gave way abruptly, which meant I'd skitter down a few inches until my heel caught something solid again. The understory wasn't thick, but there were enough brushes, brambles, and yes, more ferns, that after a dozen yards, I was covered in scratches. I tried to be smart; I tried to zigzag, in case the masked figure was taking aim. I tried to take a path that would lead me between the trunks of the massive spruce and pine. But all of that was secondary to my main goal, which was to stay upright. And staying upright meant that, no matter how fast my heart was hammering, my progress was painfully slow.

Distantly, fresh shouts broke out above me. Then a gunshot broke the forest's stillness. Dirt and decomposing leaves sprayed up a few feet to my right. I dove to the left, landed on my shoulder, and began to roll. I turned the roll into a scramble and ended up behind the bole of an enormous ponderosa pine. My brain told me to keep moving, but I felt frozen—that shot had come so close.

Up on the shoulder of the road, someone was shouting again—and you wouldn't hear any of those words in church. Farther off, an engine growled, and then the sound faded. Someone was moving through the brush higher up the ravine—leaves rustling, branches snapping.

And then Deputy Bobby's voice called, "Dash?"

I fought to control my breath. I sagged. The cold, damp leaves were like ice against my face, and they felt wonderful. Somehow, after a moment, I managed to sit up and call back, "Here!"

CHAPTER 12

Deputy Bobby helped me back up to the road. He sat me in his Pilot, told me not to get out of the car, and then jogged off—to get service, of course.

By the time he came back, I was only shaking a little. I slid out of the Pilot to meet Deputy Bobby. He cocked me a look like he didn't exactly approve of this display of initiative, but all he said was, "Some deputies are on their way. Get back in the car, please; I think you're in shock."

"I'm fine." I managed to smile as I added, "Thanks."

And honestly, I was fine. More or less. Like I said, the shaking had all but stopped. The cool air felt good—the earthiness of the moss hanging from the branches overhead, the dustiness of the broken stone underfoot, the sweet, dark pitchiness of the trees. My eyes were still playing tricks—adrenaline, and the deep shadows of the forest—and I tried adjusting my glasses. Deputy Bobby must have taken pity on me because after a few rounds of me taking off my glasses and squinting and putting them on again and squinting some more, he took the glasses from me and settled them on my face.

"Thanks," I said again, and that was when my voice decided to get wobbly. "God, thank you, Bobby. How did you—I mean, you saved my life."

"Luck. Good timing." He tucked some of my hair behind one arm of my glasses, and then he seemed to realize what he'd done and dropped his hand to his side. "You sounded serious when you said you needed to talk, and when I called you back, you didn't answer. I thought I should get back to the house."

The way he said the house sent something thrumming through me. I wasn't eager to look too closely at that particular feeling, so I said, "Dead zone."

He gave me a lopsided smile.

"Right," I said, and for some reason, I had to struggle not to cry. Somehow I managed to say, "You knew that."

"Dash, why don't you sit down?"

"No, I'm fine. I'm fine. I promise, I'm fine." A breeze lifted, branches stirred, and the trees groaned like old men. I thought I could feel a touch of the ocean on my hot cheeks. "I know I shouldn't have gone alone; please don't be mad."

And then I told him everything.

To his credit, Deputy Bobby didn't get mad. At least, he didn't shout. He didn't kick anything. He didn't get into the Pilot and drive away. Instead, he nodded. He breathed slowly and deeply. His hands opened and closed against his thighs.

It was so much worse.

"What were you thinking?"

"I don't know. I thought I'd just look around."

"Bull pucky."

Okay, that wasn't quite what he said.

Since I didn't want to spend too much time on that particular topic, I said, "But he's right, don't you think? I mean, Nate's a creep and a thief, and I'm still totally willing to believe he killed Gerry. But it was so easy to get into that safe. Whoever killed him had almost a full day when they could have gotten into his house and removed their blackmail file. And what Gerry said about Ali—"

"Ali's gone."

"What? What do you mean she's gone?"

"She disappeared, Dash. She ran away. She's been couch-surfing with friends—I guess I don't know if they were friends, but they were all part of that reclamation movement. And now she's gone."

"That's suspicious, right? That's got to mean something."

Deputy Bobby made a noise that could have meant anything.

"The sheriff has to admit it was murder now, doesn't she? I mean, the footsteps that were erased at the cliff, those blackmail files, the fact that Ali disappeared?"

"Dash—"

"I know the medical examiner has to determine the manner of death, but there's no way the sheriff is going to let this be written off as an accident, right?"

"I don't know. It's none of my business. And it's not any of yours, either."

He said it roughly—almost harshly. And the words were so unlike the Deputy Bobby I knew that it took me a minute to make sense of them, to step back and look at him, to see him, then, more closely. The red eyes. The way he folded his arms. The challenge in his face.

"Where were you?" I asked.

He shifted his weight, and the broken asphalt on the shoulder crunched under his feet.

"You said you were driving back to Hemlock House because I called. Where'd you go?"

Deputy Bobby looked past me, and when he spoke, his voice was thin and brittle, like ice about to break. "West and I talked this morning."

Even though I'd suspected it from the way he was acting, it still, somehow, felt like a surprise. "Oh God. Is that good? What happened? Are you okay?"

"Everything's fine."

"You're—" I didn't know how to phrase what I wanted to say, so I asked, "Want to talk about it?"

"There's nothing to talk about. I apologized. West accepted my apology." He adjusted his arms across his chest. He was still looking out into the trees, the moss, the ferns shaped like swords. "We're good now."

"You're good now."

"That's what I said."

But this time, I recognized the unfamiliar hostility for what it was: defensiveness. It was easy to recognize; I was feeling some of it myself. "What did you talk about?"

Something flickered in Deputy Bobby's eyes, but he said, "I told you. I apologized."

I made a noise of understanding.

His gaze flicked to me for less than a heartbeat, and then he wrenched it back to the trees again.

"Did you write down what you wanted to say to him?" I asked.

Deputy Bobby didn't answer.

"Did you?" I asked again.

"I appreciate you—"

"You didn't, did you?" The question dropped open like a trap door between us. After a moment, I said, "Of course you didn't."

Now he looked at me. A dusky flush rose under his golden-olive skin. Even in the canopy's deep shadows, his pupils looked hard and small. "I didn't need to write anything down. I just needed to apologize. We both overreacted, and now it's all over."

"You overreacted? Really? Do you remember last night?"

"I remember that this is my relationship. Mine. And I don't need your opinion or your commentary." He struggled to add, in an approximation of his normal voice, "Thank you for being worried, but I don't want to talk about this anymore."

The old Dash would have let it drop there. Heck, the old Dash never would have gotten this far in the first place. But apparently, having your entire life turned upside down and shaken like a dollhouse goes a long way toward helping you deal with your conflict avoidance patterns. Also, confronting murderers didn't hurt. So even though I tried to do what he asked, I felt myself already starting to speak.

"Big surprise," I said, "you don't want to talk about it. Well, too bad. God, why are you being such a—such a dude about this? You're so smart. Most of the time. You're so funny and kind and generous and good. And you deserve to be happy. Instead, you give me this nonsense about how everything's fine and it all blew over. Stuff like this doesn't blow over. That's why you're so unhappy!"

My shout echoed out into the trees. The branches above us shifted in the breeze, and shadows rose and fell on Deputy Bobby's face. He stared at me. The hurt in his face was already closing, hardening, turning into a wall I didn't know how to get past.

"I *am* happy," Deputy Bobby said.

"No, you're not. You don't want to move to Portland. You don't want to give up working in law enforcement. You don't want to be a doctor, or whatever you think you're supposed to do. You don't want to do any of that. And I don't know why you can't just tell him."

"I'm fine, for your information. West and I are fine."

I shook my head, and now I was the one to look away.

"You know something, Dash?" He laughed—part scoff, part scorn, and it was the first time, I realized distantly, I'd ever heard Deputy Bobby try to hurt somebody. "For someone who whines and moans about how bad he is at relationships, you're sure quick to talk about stuff you don't know anything about."

Deeper among the trees, a bird broke into flight—a flurried flap of wings that shattered the stillness. The sound of tires on pavement came next, and a sheriff's office cruiser came over the hill.

The weight of Deputy Bobby's gaze rested on me for another long moment. And then, without another word, he got in his car and left.

CHAPTER 13

I told Salk what had happened. At least, I think I told him. My body seemed to be on autopilot while my brain played back snatches of that horrible argument with Deputy Bobby. Salk looked around. He couldn't find a shell casing. He couldn't find a bullet. I think he believed me, but all my higher-level functions had come unplugged, and none of it seemed to matter. He called a tow truck. He waited with me.

Mr. Del Real, who owned Swift Lift Towing, told me someone had tampered with the alternator. I thought about how I'd parked right next to the service garage. About how Nate had disappeared in that direction after I'd tried to talk to him the first time. But it wasn't just Nate who could have done it. Ali Rivas basically had a part-time job disabling machinery. And against my will, I remembered that Jen had told me Damian was good with cars.

As Mr. Del Real was hooking up the Jeep, Salk said, "I think you're in shock. Let me take you to the medical center."

I shook my head. "I just want to go home."

Which was how, about an hour later, I ended up in bed.

A while later, the shadows had changed, deepened, and now the room was dark. I wasn't sure I'd slept. I didn't know where I'd been. Someone was knocking at the door.

"Dashiell, dear," Indira called through the wood. "Would you mind opening the door? We're all a bit worried about you."

I thought about ignoring her. But that had never worked with the Last Picks, so I said, "I'm fine. I just need some time alone."

"Did you hear that?" Millie said. It was like she was standing right next to the bed, by the way. "Did you hear his voice? He's definitely NOT FINE."

"I am fine," I said. "I'm totally fine. I'll be down for dinner."

The strained silence on the other side of the door told me I'd made a mistake. I glanced at the clock. It was after nine, which seemed impossible—had I really spent all day in here?

Apparently so, because now my brain told me that my bladder situation was approaching a nuclear meltdown.

"Dash." This time it was Fox. "Indira made you—well, she made you pretty much everything. There's a hamburger. There's a quesadilla. There's eight-cheese pasta, because remember you told her that four cheeses weren't enough? And where are we at on the cakes?"

Indira's answer was muffled.

"We're up to five," Fox announced with an overabundance of cheer. "Don't you want to know what they are?"

Before I could stop myself, I asked, "Is one of them spice cake?"

"Yes, one of them is definitely spice cake."

"Is one of them peanut butter cheesecake?"

"Uh, sure."

"What about the apple one that she makes in the skillet?"

"I guess you'll have to come see," Fox said.

That part wasn't quite as appealing.

"Besides," Fox added, "Millie is going to cry if you don't let us make sure you're okay, and you don't want Millie to cry, do you?"

I did not. I had the feeling that the phrase "gale-force winds" would be involved.

When I opened the door, the three of them were standing right outside my room: Indira's face was grave; Fox was aiming at cheerful and landing closer to manic; and Millie—

Millie burst into tears as soon as she saw me. "Oh Dash," she wailed (and one of my ear drums ruptured in the pressure differential), "YOU'RE SO SAD!"

She crashed into me with a hug, her tiny body shaking against me.

It was strangely easier to deal with this than with—well, with everything else. I patted her back. Then I rubbed her back. Then I patted her back some more. I made soothing sounds. I said all sorts of idiotic things like "Don't cry," and "Everything's fine," and worst of all, "I promise I'm not sad, Millie. Really."

And as I did, I had nowhere to look but at Keme. He sat on a sideboard, bare feet swinging in the air as he glared at me, his expression set to death-by-incineration.

Finally, Millie calmed down. She hugged me one final time and stepped back, wiping her face.

"Deputy Salkanovic said you might be in shock," Indira said, but it was more of a question.

And Fox, with a disturbingly keen look in their eyes, added, "And Bobby's not answering his phone."

"Dash," Millie asked, "what happened?"

So, I told them: Nate, and then the Jeep dying, and then Deputy Bobby. As much as I could tell them, I guess. Because there were parts of it—what I hadn't said, what I'd wanted to say—that I kept buried. Because they didn't matter. They never had, I realized. It had all been in my head.

Millie started crying again, of course.

"I'm sure it's not as bad as it seems," Indira said, rubbing Millie's shoulders. "You had a disagreement, that's all."

Fox couldn't quite meet my eyes. "I'm so sorry, Dash." And then, in what must have been a last-ditch effort: "But that's good news about Ali, isn't it? I mean, she's on the run, which means she's hiding from something.

And someone tried to kill you again, which is *very* promising. Maybe next we can—"

I shook my head. "I'm done with that. Deputy Bobby was right: it's none of my business, and I shouldn't have gotten involved in the first place."

Fox looked like they wanted to argue about that, but after a moment, they shut their mouth.

"Let's go downstairs and have something to eat," Indira said. "We'll all feel better after we get some food in us."

"I'm not hungry," I said.

Millie let out a sob.

Fox glared at me.

Keme's feet stilled in the air.

Indira's eyes were wide, as though I'd slapped her.

I mumbled, "I, uh, suppose I could eat something." Jerking a thumb toward the room, I said, "Let me wash my hands."

"You're not going to lock yourself in your room again, are you?" Fox asked.

Millie sniffled. "Is this one of your sadness baths?"

"No," I said. "And no. And I don't even know what a sadness bath is."

"We'll see you downstairs," Indira said, and mercifully, she herded the others toward the stairs.

I peed. I washed my hands. I considered the creature from the Black Lagoon who had appeared in my mirror. I honestly hadn't known, until right now, that eyes could come in that shade of red.

For a moment, the pain threatened to overwhelm me: how terribly everything had gone with Bobby; how much I'd hurt him, because I'd been selfish, because I'd let my own feelings take control; the fact that, no matter what happened now, our friendship wouldn't be the same. He'd move. And maybe, for a while, we'd keep trying. But the gulf—physical and emotional— would be too great. I didn't know how to deal with that much pain—didn't want to think about what it meant, that it could hurt so much. So, I stuffed it all down inside me somewhere, and I let myself out of the bathroom.

The blur of movement came so fast that I didn't have time to respond. The blow to my head rocked me back, and I stumbled into the doorjamb. I stared at Keme in disbelief. He hadn't hit me hard, not exactly, but he hadn't been roughhousing either. His dark hair hung loose, and combined with the glint in his eyes, it made him look feral. He held my gaze for a moment, and then he pointed toward the front of the house.

"What the heck—" I began.

Before I could finish, Keme kicked me in the shin. Even though he was barefoot, it hurt, and I hopped as I massaged my leg. "Ow! What's wrong with you?"

He stabbed his finger at the front of the house again.

"Fine, fine, I'm going. But you don't have to be a jerk—"

I didn't get to finish the sentence; Keme tried to cuff me again. This time, my reactions were faster, and I managed to avoid the blow.

He was still glaring at me. And, I realized, he was about to cry. Again, he pointed to the front of the house.

"I don't know what that means—"

"Go talk to him, you donkey!"

I stared at Keme.

Keme stared back. His chest was heaving, and he dashed at his eyes. His voice was rocky as he said, "God, why do you always have to be such an idiot?"

I didn't know what to say. I didn't know what to do. In all fairness to myself, I'd never heard Keme talk before. (And, honestly, it was a great question.) All I could think about was his voice. It wasn't an adult's voice, not yet. But it was pleasantly masculine, with a little gravel in it that was going to drive the girls (or boys, or whoever) crazy.

"You're talking to me," I said.

"This is what I mean: it's like you've got sand in your head. Did you hear me? Go talk to Bobby. Right now."

"You've never talked to me."

"Dash!"

"Well, I'm sorry. I'm still processing. Wait, why are you talking to me now?"

"Because, dingus, this is the first time I've had to fix things. Go. Talk. To. Bobby."

"Uh, no?"

He tried to kick me again.

"Knock it off," I said. "Bobby doesn't want to talk to me. He made that perfectly clear today. He doesn't want me around. He doesn't want me to be involved in his life. He doesn't want my friendship."

"Did he say that?"

The question felt like a trap. Finally, I said, "No." Then I held up a finger and added, "It's complicated for adults. I know you don't understand, but I promise, I already tried talking to Bobby, and he made it clear that he doesn't want to talk to me."

Keme gave me a look, and it was less than flattering. "God, this is what I tell Millie all the time: you really are as stupid as you look."

"Hey—"

"Why do you even wear those dumb glasses if you're not going to be the useful kind of nerd?"

"Okay, rewind. In the first place, these glasses are actually hip right now, and I am the useful kind of nerd because I still know all the secret passages in *GoldenEye*—"

"Go talk to Bobby!"

"He doesn't want to talk to me. I tried, and he shut me down. Why would I put myself through that again—"

"Because not everybody knows how to talk about their feelings!" The shout hung in the air. Keme looked away from me and pushed his hair back unsteadily. In a softer voice, he said, "You live your whole life in words, Dash. And that's great. But not everybody's like that."

I tried to find an answer for that. More words, I thought, and a part of me wanted to laugh. Just a teensy-weensy bit of hysterics. Hadn't Deputy Bobby tried to tell me the same thing? He'd told me about his dad. He'd told me about his mom. He'd told me about what happened when he tried to talk to West.

Keme's gaze had come back to me, uncertainty written in the lines around his eyes as he tried to read me.

"I liked you better when you didn't talk," I told him.

He scowled, but only for an instant. Then a smile slanted across his face, and he made a very, very, very rude gesture.

CHAPTER 14

Deputy Bobby (and West) lived in a shake-sided walk-up. It was a four-plex, two up and two down, and it looked old and comfortable and probably in need of a safety inspection. Their second-floor apartment was dark when I rode up to the building, and I decided that was a sign that I should probably go home.

I didn't, though—and not because Keme would beat me up if I did. (Not entirely because of that, anyway.) I slowed my bike, hopped off, and walked it to the stairs. The blue fixed-gear Deputy Bobby had given me had carried me across town without a problem, tires whispering on the pavement, the town itself reduced to a geometry of shadowy shapes and distant lights. Like signal fires, I thought, that someone had forgotten to put out. Just me out here, alone with the sweet cedars and the brine of the ocean and the storm-spin of my thoughts. And now, as I looked up the dark chute of the stairs, I thought alone was right. Because in the dark, we're all alone.

The treads creaked under me as I started up. A few of them sagged precipitously. My hand whispered against the rail, a noise that was almost a hiss. When I got to Deputy Bobby's door, I listened. It was one thing, I realized, to argue in the heat of the moment. Now, standing here, I fought the urge to put out a hand, steady myself, fight the sensation that the world was tilting perilously to one side. Also, a little less poetically, I fought the urge to ralph all over the doormat.

Someone, though—definitely not me—was finally brave enough to knock.

When the door opened, I knew it was Deputy Bobby standing there, even though he was only a shadow. I knew the shape of him. I knew that crisply male scent. I knew what his breathing sounded like. It was what he would sound like, part of me thought dizzily, if I woke in the night.

He turned and walked back into the apartment and left the door open behind him.

After what felt like a long time, I followed him.

It was even darker inside, and I had to move slowly. I'd been in their apartment before. Plenty of times, actually. Because we were friends. And I knew the shape of the rooms, the layout. But tonight, in the dark, everything was transformed. Unfamiliar shadows loomed on every side, turning the space into a labyrinth. The rational part of my mind knew it was simply the preparations for the move—boxes stacked along the walls, making the rooms shrink, and displaced furniture, and other shadows I couldn't unravel. I caught a glimpse of the kitchen. Cabinet doors stood open to reveal empty shelves. The little water bowl marked Kylie (their dog) was missing.

My sneaker came down on something that crinkled. I almost kept moving. And then I stopped, crouched, felt across the bare boards until I swept up the papers. The only light in the apartment filtered in from outside—a pallid, lunar glow. I angled the papers toward the window, and I could make out the words.

West, it began in Deputy Bobby's now familiar handwriting. His letters always tilted a little to the right. He made fat o's and squashed a's. The letters were tightly together, joined, controlled.

I knew I should stop reading.

West, I need to tell you something, and I'm sorry that I didn't do this sooner because I know I've made it worse by waiting. I'm sorry that I've been a coward. I care so much about you, and you mean so much to me. And more than anything, I want you to be happy.

The letter continued; I didn't. In part, because of the rawness of the emotion on the page. In part, because I couldn't blink fast enough to clear my eyes. I folded the letter as neatly as I could and clutched it in one hand. I thought, maybe, he would want it later.

Bobby sat on the sofa, where not so long ago, I'd put him to bed after he'd had a little too much to drink. He had his elbows on his knees, his face in his hands. Across his back, the light that passed between the blinds threw skeletal stripes.

I eased down onto the sofa next to him. The old, familiar terror was cranking its engine inside me. I couldn't seem to take a deep breath. Black spots danced in my vision. That I would make a mistake. That I would do something wrong. Even though the rational part of me knew this moment wasn't about me. Even though that rational part knew that Bobby had other things he was focused on—not my bumbling attempts to comfort him. My time in Hastings Rock might have made it easier to confront murderers, but when it came to relationships, I was apparently still the same old Dash.

The rational part of me knew that this was the primitive part of my brain, that this was the part that feared rejection, feared being cast out of the tribe, being alone in the dark, without fire or friend. Plenty of therapists had told me so. And I knew to take deep breaths. To sit with the discomfort. To accept. I was probably still going to be in the process of accepting when I blacked out from lack of oxygen.

But this was Bobby. And for him, maybe, I could be more than myself. For a few moments, I could be braver. Better.

Somehow, I managed to say, "Are you okay?"

He was silent. And he was still. And then, head in his hands, he shook out a slow no.

"Do you want to talk about it?"

He shook his head again.

A minute passed. And then another. The apartment was cold, and next to me, Bobby was warm.

His body hitched—a tiny movement. Barely anything at all. Because, of course, even now he was trying to hold all the pieces together.

It was like someone had opened a door in my mind. I knew what to do. Maybe for the first time in my entire life, I knew what to do in a social situation. And the terror rushed back like smoke: choking, blinding.

The coward inside me offered options: I could make an excuse and leave. Bobby would probably be grateful, that treacherous little voice inside me said. He'd probably want me to leave. Or I could sit here and do nothing. That would be enough, to provide companionship, to let him know he wasn't alone. He'd be grateful.

But I'd know. For the rest of my life, I'd know that I could have done more. And I would regret that, for Bobby, I hadn't been brave enough.

I scooted closer. I slipped my arm around Bobby. His body hitched again, and then he tensed, like he might push me away, stand, leave. I tightened my arm around him. I'm here, I said, even though I didn't speak. I'm here.

Slowly, by degrees, the tension in his body slackened. His head came to rest on my shoulder. His cheek was fever hot, even through my shirt.

I'm here, I said again, the best way I could. I'm here. You're not alone.

CHAPTER 15

Eventually, I convinced Deputy Bobby to let me drive him back to Hemlock House. It was a war of attrition more than anything else; he didn't argue—heck, he didn't even really respond. But with enough cajoling, I got him into the Pilot, and I loaded my bike in the back, and we drove home. I made sure he was settled in his room, and then I started toward mine.

Indira was waiting for me in the hall.

I checked my phone. It was after eleven. "What are you still doing up?"

"How are you?"

"Terrible."

She nodded and took my arm. "Let's get you something to eat."

Before I could protest, she led me toward the stairs.

Maybe I should have been surprised to find the Last Picks in the servants' dining room, but I wasn't. Fox looked at me soberly. Millie had a bewildering, red-eyed hopefulness. And Keme glowered at me, apparently under the assumption that I had, as usual, screwed everything up. He wasn't wrong. They looked like they'd been picking at the cakes Indira had made in a frenzy of worry-baking (we'd gone from five cakes to ten, so she'd been busy while I was gone, and I spotted a pumpkin trifle that, if I'd been feeling better, I would have attacked like a cartoon piranha.)

After planting me in a seat, Indira headed for the kitchen.

"What happened?" Millie asked.

"I don't know," I said. "I think he and West might have broken up, but he's—he's not in a good place. He didn't want to talk."

Millie nodded and immediately started crying again.

Keme doubled down on his glower.

"You did a kind thing," Fox said.

I thought of the fight I'd picked with Bobby. The argument. My insistence that he shouldn't let his problems with West blow over. My smile had a lot of sharp edges when I asked, "Did I?"

"Yes, you did. Bobby shouldn't be alone tonight."

I nodded.

In a surprisingly kind voice, Fox added, "And whatever happened between Bobby and West, it's not your fault."

"It feels like it is."

"I'm sure it does. But you might ask Bobby, after some time has passed, what he thinks. My guess is that he'll tell you the same thing the rest of us will: that we all need friends who will tell us the truth. Especially the hard truths."

Which I agreed with, in theory, although I'd have preferred not to be the one with the hard truths.

Keme broke through my thoughts by saying, "Like, for example, you're an idiot."

"What did I do now?" I asked.

Keme looked at Millie, who was wiping her eyes with a napkin.

"Millie," I said. "It's okay. Bobby's going to be all right, and West will be all right. People break up all the time. They'll get over it."

"I know," she said, but she was crying harder. "That's what makes it so sad."

I had no idea how to respond to that, but before I had to, Indira returned from the kitchen. Along with the promised eight-cheese pasta, she was carrying one of her sheet pan dinners—chicken thighs roasted with a medley of vegetables (I noticed approvingly an abundance of potatoes). It smelled amazing. It looked amazing. And, best of all, it wasn't soup. (For whatever reason, autumn brings out people's latent soup-making tendencies. For, like, three months, I have to be on high alert.)

I didn't feel hungry, but as soon as I started eating, I was ravenous. Keme made a face. Fox rolled their eyes. Millie was apparently so fascinated (probably like the viewers of *Animal Planet*) that she forgot about crying.

Indira eyed me and then said to Fox, "It's flattering, but I was almost positive there were bones in those chicken thighs."

"Maybe he'll choke," Fox said with disturbing optimism.

I paused my chicken-devouring long enough to say, "Change of subject."

"We still can't find Ali Rivas," Millie said. "Keme and I looked everywhere."

I had to pause again. "What?"

"We checked her apartment, we checked the student union building, we checked EVERYWHERE."

Fox discreetly held up two fingers and mouthed, *Two places.*

I wanted to point out that Ali's disappearance—like so much about her that I'd heard over the last few days—simply didn't make sense. Instead, I went for "We don't need to find Ali—"

"Of course we do," Indira said. "Someone murdered that man, and even though he was a terrible human being, that's not right."

Fox nodded. "And it'll be a loose thread if we don't. Can you imagine if they ended an episode of *Law & Order* that way? Oh wait—they did! No, did they?"

"I have no idea what's happening right now," I said as I brushed aside parsnip and red onion to get at another piece of perfectly roasted potato. "But this isn't an episode of *Law & Order*, and it's not our responsibility to find whoever killed Gerry."

"But you LOVE catching killers," Millie said—unnecessarily, in my opinion.

"No," I said. "I don't. I love minding my own business. I love naps. I love— isn't there a German word for when you lie around in your pajamas all day and eat pretzels?"

Keme gave Fox a look.

"It's called self-delusion," Fox explained. "People are capable of tremendous amounts of it. It gets worse the older you get."

"I'm not delusional," I began. "I'm perfectly aware—"

And then I stopped.

Because I saw it.

Gerry's too dark hair and goatee. Gerry's creams and lotions and cosmetics. What we'd been told: that Gerry had liked going after younger men. Maybe too young.

It was just like my Will Gower story: I'd been so focused on what I thought I knew that I'd made an assumption. The evidence had been right in front of me, but I'd misinterpreted it because I'd thought I'd known what it meant. Which, to be fair, I was in good company—it was a mystery novel classic for a reason.

"I know how we can find the killer," I said. "And I know how we can lure them out. And I know how we can make it impossible for them to resist. But I'm going to need your help." I took a breath. "Have you ever heard of somatotropin?"

CHAPTER 16

The next day passed in a blur. I drove all over town, talking to people, asking questions, requesting records, doing my due diligence to make sure my hunch was right. A large amount of that time—an ungodly amount, to be perfectly frank—I spent at the sheriff's station. The rest of the Last Picks were busy too—Millie at Chipper, Indira at the fishermen's market, Fox visiting studios and galleries. Keme was in charge of keeping an eye on Bobby, who seemed determined to avoid me at all costs (he literally turned around one time and walked in the other direction). Not that I blamed him. I was the one who'd goaded him into—into whatever he'd done. He was right to be angry with me.

That evening, I tried to stay busy. The house was painfully quiet. There was no sign of Bobby (and he wasn't answering his phone), and Indira had long since retired to the coach house. I tried to play *Super Smash Bros*, but I kept getting killed. (Okay, I probably would have gotten killed even if I hadn't been so distracted.) I tried to write, but I just sat there, staring at a blank document, cursing my ancestors (specifically, my parents). I tried to read, but my eyes kept falling shut. So I could concentrate. Because I was thinking. With my eyes shut.

A noise woke me, and for a single, disoriented moment, I didn't know where I was. Then I made out the familiar shapes: the chandelier, the TV, the built-in shelves. The billiard room's darkness was softened by the ambient glow of LED power lights on various electronics, but it was dark enough. When I checked my phone, the clock said it was past two in the morning. The sound came again—the squeak of rubber soles on the hardwood floor. I fumbled with the lamp and winced as light bloomed.

When I could see again, I was looking at Jen Kang, from the surf camp. She was dressed in black. And she was holding a gun.

I had a certain amount of self-interest invested in the gun, but I forced myself to look at her face, to see the signs. The overdeveloped jaw was the clearest one, but her brow as well, and the acne scars were there too. Her free hand was pressed to her thigh. A big hand. I should have noticed that before.

"Hi, Jen," I said.

She moved her mouth soundlessly once. Sweat glistened on her forehead, even though the house was cool. When she tried again, she managed to get the words out, but they were rough. "Where is it?"

"Where's what?"

"Don't do that!" The hand with the gun wavered, and in a more controlled voice, she said, "Don't. The files. Where are they?"

"What files?"

"Gerry's blackmail files. I know he had duplicates, and I know you found them. Where are they?"

"That's why you—"

"Yes." The word sounded thick in her throat. "Yes, that's why I killed him. Because he was blackmailing me."

"You know, just one time, I would like to be the one who explains everything."

Jen, though, was on a roll. "The weasel waited until he knew he had me hooked. We'd started construction on the surf camp. I'd invested everything I had, plus the loans. I thought he was just a kooky old guy who liked to look at the eye candy. And then one night, he came to my apartment and told me."

"He knew you were using—"

"HGH. Yeah. He figured it out somehow."

I should have figured it out sooner too. Not only because Gerry's laptop had showed a recent search for somatotropin, another name for human growth hormone. At the time, I'd written it off as part of Gerry's quest to stay young. But I should have noticed it in Jen. Her age. Her attempts to stay competitive. The acromegaly—the continued growth of bones in her face and hands and, I was sure, her feet too. It was a distinctive look. And, of course, any business partner of Gerry's should have been at the top of my list.

"I tried to blow it off," Jen said, "but I didn't fool him. And then I tried to explain. He didn't understand. It's hard enough to be a woman in this sport. It's even harder to be queer. And every year, it's a little harder to get up on the board, a little harder to stay up, a little harder to do everything that used to be easy. It wasn't too bad when we did the surf camp once a year; I could get by. But a permanent surf camp? Running this place year-round? I'm the owner. I'm the lead instructor. Who's going to come if I'm just another old lady trying to relive my glory days."

I had my own doubts about those glory days—my guess was that Jen had always had an excuse for why she needed *just a little help*. But that wasn't really the point. I said, "And Gerry wanted you to pay."

"To pay? He wanted everything. He was going to take all of it. Sure, I'd own the surf camp in name, but it would be his. He was going to turn it into—into a kiddie park. An attraction. One more stupid perk for his planned community. He was going to scrap all the stuff that made it important, all the stuff I'd worked for. He told me to forget about all that gay stuff; he had a better idea. Like that was the end of the story. Everything I'd worked for, and he was going to take it away. If he talked, my reputation would be ruined. Nobody would come here to learn how to surf, not from me. It would be over before it started. He was going to ruin everything."

"And then you saw your chance."

Jen shook her head—not at my words, but at something else. A memory maybe. Or some part of her that still protested. "He was sloshed. You saw him.

You saw how he was; he couldn't keep his hands off you. And I'd been thinking all day about when Nate tackled him at the beach. Seeing that, seeing Gerry go down, seeing him get hurt." She stopped. She flexed the fingers of her free hand. "I couldn't stop thinking about it. About how good it felt. And then it happened again. Bobby. Good old Bobby. He got right in Gerry's face and let that ancient fart have it. God, it felt *so* good. I thought, this is how it would feel if he died. This is how it would feel, like this." Her voice took on an unbelieving note. "And then he walked straight out toward the cliffs. It was like—like someone meant for it to happen. Like it was supposed to be this way. Everybody else was busy with the party. Nobody noticed when I left. Gerry didn't even know I was following him. He was angry. He was embarrassed—humiliated, I guess. I could tell from how he walked. He didn't have any idea where he was going—he was just walking, just trying to get away. He walked right up to the edge of the cliff. He was swaying; he could hardly stay upright. I didn't even have to push him that hard."

The silence that came after was thicker, deeper. She was looking at me, but I didn't think she was seeing me. And then her eyes focused, and her expression flattened out until she looked like a different person. Her fingers flexed around the grip of the gun.

"Where are the files?"

"It wasn't just the drugs, though, was it?" I tried to keep my eyes on her face, but the gun kept pulling my gaze back. "That wasn't the only thing he had on you."

She pulled her head back to the edge of the lamp's light. Shadows swallowed up her eyes.

"Because you killed—"

"Yes." The word was small and fragile. "Yes, I killed Ali."

Once, I thought. Just once I wanted to get a chance to explain.

"It was an accident. We were arguing. I was so angry." She stopped. She was nothing more than a silhouette now, but the dry click of her throat was clear in the quiet. "She wouldn't get up. And there was so much blood." Her voice frayed on the last word, and silence rolled in on another dark tide. "I don't know how he found out. He said he had evidence."

"You faked the—"

"The vandalism. Yes." Her voice was growing stronger. "For weeks. That was his idea too."

"To make sure people thought she was still alive. That's why no one could figure out how the cameras kept getting disabled, how she kept sneaking past the surfers who were standing guard. Because you were doing it, so that when she finally did 'disappear'—"

"I'd have the perfect alibi." Her breathing was smoothing out. That dry click came again in her throat. "After…Gerry, I thought I'd done everything perfectly. I made sure I didn't leave any footprints. And I knew, with the party as wild as it had been, no one would notice I'd been gone. It had only been a few minutes, and if I nudged the right person, I was sure they'd 'remember' I'd been with them all night. Once the police had left, I broke a few windows. It was almost dawn by that point. I didn't know the medical examiner had said it was an accident; I thought the sheriff would make the connection to Ali."

"Jen, why don't you put down the gun?" I asked. "You don't want to do this. Bobby's your friend. Keme too. This isn't the Jen they know and care about. They wouldn't want you to do this—none of your friends would."

The silence was a held breath. And then she gave a strange, tilt-a-whirl laugh. "They wouldn't be my friends if they knew the truth, though, would they?"

"That's not true—"

"We're done talking, Mr. Dane. I want those files. And then I'll leave, and no one has to get hurt."

She wasn't a particularly good liar; her tone slipped at the end, and I wondered how she'd been able to get away with everything for as long as she had. Then Jen gestured with the gun, and my nerves almost failed me. I could shout. I could try to run. But even if Jen wasn't a crack shot, she only had to hit me once to kill me, and she was close enough that I didn't want to risk it.

Hands raised in surrender, I stood and moved toward the billiards table. Jen followed, keeping the gun trained on me. Her hand had steadied; any doubt or fear had vanished. She was going to get what she wanted, whatever the cost. I figured that had been Jen's way her whole life—this was just the next level. As we moved out of the ring of lamplight, I watched each step, trying not to trip over the shadowy shapes of rugs and end tables and potted plants and who knew whatever else. You could say one thing about Victorian homes: they weren't short on junk.

"The files—" Jen said.

"I hid them. I thought this might happen. I thought someone might hear I'd found them. Someone might come looking." I took a breath. "How'd you find out?"

"Keme," she said with a voice of grim satisfaction. "He couldn't wait to tell Damian. Keme has a bit of a man-crush on you, in case you weren't aware. And Damian wanted to know everything he could about you."

I wasn't sure Jen had her facts right—I put Keme near the top of my list of people who seemed to be annoyed by my very existence—but then, Jen didn't seem like she was playing with a full set of marbles. Before I had to respond to her comment, though, my hip bumped the billiards table. I found the rail and slid my hand along it, counting the diamonds (mother-of-pearl inset into the aged mahogany).

"What are you doing?" Jen demanded. "This better not be a trick."

"It's not a trick. This is an old house. There are a lot of secrets. I told you I had to hide the files." I found the correct diamond; it moved slightly under my finger. "I'm going to press this, and a panel in the wall is going to open." I gave a nervous laugh that sounded more like a wheeze. "I don't want to startle you."

"Which panel?" Jen said. "Where?"

"Over there. Next to the cue rack."

She gave me a long, considering look. And then she said, "I'm telling you, this better not be a trick."

"No tricks."

A second passed. Then another. "All right."

I pressed the diamond. The concealed latch *snicked*.

Jen gave a nervous laugh and peered through the gloom, obviously trying to tell if the panel had opened. "That's it?"

"That's it. The documents are in there."

She shifted her weight. And then her voice hardened, and she said, "Open it."

"I'm telling you the truth—"

"Open it right now. You open it. I'm not going to—I'm not going to fall for it, whatever it is."

"Fall for what?"

"Whatever it is!" The shout ripped through the darkness. "You open it!"

I showed my hands in surrender again and moved over to the panel. With the latch released, it had opened a quarter inch—barely enough, really, for me to get my fingertips in the seam. I eased the secret door open. Indira had shown me this one; God only knew how she'd learned about it. On the other side, absolute darkness waited for me.

"Quit stalling!"

I found the inside handle of the door—a simple old brass knob. It didn't even have anything cool about it like a poison pin that killed you if you turned it the wrong way. And then, after a mental three-count, I darted through the doorway and yanked the door shut behind me.

Hands caught me by the shoulders, forcing me to the floor. I squawked, and a hand went over my mouth.

"Hey!" Jen shouted. And then, outrage turning to fury, "Hey!"

I squawked again.

The hand tightened over my mouth, and Bobby whispered, "Quiet."

This had definitely not been part of the plan.

"You've got two seconds before I start shooting!" Jen shouted. She pounded on the paneling. "Open this door! Open—"

Sirens blatted in the distance, and then the sheriff's voice ordered, "Drop your weapon! Drop it! Drop the gun!"

Jen's silence had a frozen quality.

"Drop the gun!" the sheriff shouted.

Something thunked against one of the thick rugs.

"On the floor! Hands behind your head!"

Through the old house's thick walls came the sounds of movement. And then, voice still tight, the sheriff said, "All clear. You can come out now." Without missing a beat, she began to mirandize Jen.

For one heartbeat more, Bobby and I lay on the floor: his body wrapped around mine, the weight and heat of him like the world's best electric blanket. He breathed out slightly as he pulled his hand from my mouth, and the infinitesimal tension of his body eased.

"What," I asked "are *you* doing here?"

CHAPTER 17

The sheriff's station wasn't going to win any awards for interior decorating. The sheriff's office itself was nice enough, if you were into that sort of thing: a desk, a computer, plaques for awards and recognitions, photos of two children (a boy with a gap-toothed smile, and a girl who could have been Sheriff Acosta in miniature). The blinds were down, not that there was much to see this time of night. It would have been nice, of course, to see one more sunrise before the sheriff executed me, probably with her bare hands.

After the sheriff had arrested Jen, everything had happened with that hybrid mix of urgency and delay that seemed to accompany anything official. More deputies arrived. Jen was taken away. Deputy Bobby and I were separated, and deputies took our statements. The sheriff hadn't said a word to either of us, but she hadn't looked happy. And when the deputies had finally seemed to decide that they'd had enough of Indira's coffee and cookies, the sheriff told them to take me with them. And now here I was. Sitting in her office. I wondered if I'd get a blindfold and a last cigarette. Oh, or a last meal.

The door opened, and Sheriff Acosta entered. She looked tired, but then, I looked like a wreck. (The floor of that secret passage had been dusty, and apparently, tricking a confession out of a murderer makes me super sweaty. The result was that I looked like a walking dust bunny.) Maybe something similar crossed the sheriff's mind, because as she settled into her seat, I thought she was trying not to smile. Then, in her most official voice, she said, "Mr. Dane."

"Don't punish Bobby."

Sheriff Acosta stared at me.

"I mean please," I said. "Please don't punish him. Or arrest him. Or whatever."

She kept staring.

"I didn't tell him about my plan. He wasn't part of it. And he didn't know I was going to call you and—please. He wasn't supposed to be involved." Although, since Deputy Bobby had been inside that secret passage, waiting for me—and, doubtless, watching through the hidden peepholes that looked in on the billiard room—I had a good idea who had told him I might need help. "Please don't take it out on him."

"It's sheriff's office policy not to discuss ongoing investigations—"

"Please!" And then genius struck. "I'll go to the media! I'll talk to the press! I tell them he caught Jen, and he'll be a national hero, and if you go after him—"

"For God's sake, Dash, knock it off." It wasn't quite a shout. She didn't even sound angry—at the end of her rope, maybe, but with a kind of good-humored vexation that took me by surprise. "I'm not going to do anything to Bobby. You should be more worried about him killing you, by the way. He's not happy with you. And, for the record, neither am I."

I caught myself before I could continue my in-defense-of-Deputy-Bobby rant. And then I said, "He's not in trouble?"

"I'd like to give him a stern talking-to, but there's not much point if he's still planning on leaving."

The best I could come up with was "Oh." Was Deputy Bobby still leaving? I didn't know. I didn't know anything, actually. He'd avoided me the day before, in spite of my best efforts to check on him. Maybe he'd changed his mind.

Maybe he and West had patched things up. Or maybe he just couldn't stay here any longer. Maybe he was going to move to California and be a beach bum.

Whatever the sheriff saw on my face softened her expression. "And since you seem to be so invested in Bobby's future, I'll tell you that I asked him to reconsider. Again. Tonight. He's a good deputy, and he's got a lot of potential, and aside from his taste in men, he seems to have his head screwed on straight." There were a lot of ways to take that last sentence, but before I could try to decipher it, the sheriff continued, "Mr. Dane, we need to have a talk."

This was it, I thought. Maybe she wasn't going to execute me personally (no last meal, tragically), but there'd be an arrest, charges of some kind, punishment. She'd warned me, after all, not to interfere with her investigations.

"I…understand that you have been a significant part of several recent investigations. And I'd be ungrateful not to acknowledge that, in some instances, you've helped identify culprits who might, otherwise, have evaded justice. And I also want to acknowledge that even though you did something stupid tonight, you tried to…involve the sheriff's office."

Which was true. I had. All that time I'd spent at the sheriff's station? I'd been convincing Sheriff Acosta to keep an eye on the house. Personally. And when Jen had shown up in the middle of the night and snuck into the house dressed in all black, well, the sheriff had, naturally, been curious. Curious enough, in fact, that she'd overheard my conversation with Jen and Jen's confession. So, in the most technical sense, my plan had worked. Perfectly. I was going to keep repeating that phrase because I wasn't sure Deputy Bobby or Sheriff Acosta saw it that way.

"If you're going to arrest me—"

"This is a small town," Sheriff Acosta said over me.

But that was it. I watched her. And then I felt a tiny smile. "Is this a version of 'This town ain't big enough for the both of us'?"

"No, Dash. This is me telling you we've got to find a way to live together. I don't want civilians jeopardizing my investigations. But I'd be an idiot not to recognize that you've been an asset—albeit, of the pain-in-my-rear kind. And I'm not an idiot. From what I understand, you're planning on staying. Is that right?"

I didn't answer. I'd thought—well, I'd thought something. But I'd thought a lot of things. And I was starting to suspect I hadn't been right about any of them.

Once again, that look of compassion softened Sheriff Acosta's face. "Well, I'm not planning on going anywhere. And if you're going to be here, then we need to find a way to do things so that I don't have to arrest you, and you don't make the sheriff's office look like a horse's behind."

(She didn't say *behind*.)

I said cautiously, "I'm not planning on getting caught up in any more murders."

For some reason, that made her laugh. "Maybe not. But you do seem to...attract them." She closed her mouth, considering me, and then said, "You know, Vivienne and Sheriff Jakes had an arrangement. It was fairly simple. When Sheriff Jakes had a difficult case, he asked Vivienne for help. And if Vivienne could help, she did."

"Like partners."

"More like a consultant."

It wasn't unprecedented; law enforcement hired all sorts of experts (and quasi-experts, like psychics and hypnotists and dog therapists). And Vivienne had certainly done her fair share of collaborating with law enforcement around the world, not just in Hastings Rock. The sheriff's offer was a fair one. It was more than fair, actually. It was downright generous. And she was doing it not because she had to, but because she was a good sheriff, and she wanted this town to be a good place to live. For everyone. Even me.

"I'm not Vivienne Carver," I said. "I don't know how much help I'll be."

"Just say yes, Dash," she said. "I'm tired, and I've still got to tell my best deputy that I think he's making a huge mistake."

I thought I had an idea who that was, and it made me smile. "Yes."

"Great. We'll work out the details later." She paused. "Consultant, Dash. Not partner."

I nodded.

"Not cowboy."

A grin slipped out. "I understand, Sheriff."

As she shook my hand, she met my gaze and held it and said, "He is making a mistake, you know. I'd appreciate it if you could help him see reason on this."

"I'm not sure I'm the right person to help. I don't think he wants any more advice from me."

She was still holding my hand, and she tilted her head, as though she were trying to see the bottom of something that was just out of sight.

"Dash," she finally said, "he doesn't want advice."

CHAPTER 18

It was a perfect Halloween night. Crisply cold, the sky full of stars and clear and hard as glass. The breeze was low, twisting through the hemlocks with the sound of a great scroll being unfurled, carrying the salt of the sea. Indira brewed an enormous pot's worth of hot cider, and Hemlock House was warm and bright and full of the scent of cinnamon and the sweet tang of apples.

And the trick-or-treaters didn't stop coming.

As the most recent pack of them retreated (this group consisted of a witch, a zombie, two princesses, and a genuine masterpiece of a costume: a dinosaur wearing a fedora), I said, "I thought Hastings Rock was a small town."

After closing the door behind them, we retreated to the reception room. We never used it, but it was conveniently located next to the front door, and there was enough seating for all of us. Plus Millie had hung about a million square yards of "spider webs" all over the main floor, so getting anywhere else in the house was an endeavor.

Keme, dressed in his "skeleton in a suit" costume again, gave me a disparaging look as he opened a fresh bag of candy and emptied it into the pumpkin-shaped bowl we were using. I went for one of the fun-sized Butterfingers, but he beat me to it. And to the next one. And the third.

"Hey!"

He was grinning as he passed me the bowl. (No Butterfingers left, I'll have you know.)

"It *is* a small town," Millie said in answer to my earlier statement. Her '80s workout costume had made a second appearance, and the only good part of the night had been watching its effect on Keme. The boy had walked into two doors (yes, two separate, distinct, totally different doors); spilled his soda when he'd tried to take a drink without, you know, actually putting the can to his mouth; and flipped right over a hassock. (Fox had to tell me it was a hassock and not a footstool.) "And Vivienne always gave out the best candy on Halloween. Plus the house is spooky, but it's GOOD spooky. Every kid in the area comes here on Halloween."

Which, thank God, they'd warned me about in advance. We'd spent the day recovering from everything with Jen. Deputy Bobby was, technically, still staying at Hemlock House, but that seemed to be more in theory than in practice. I hadn't seen him since the deputies had separated us the night before. My occasional texts making sure he was okay had been answered with the kind of short, declarative sentences that made me want to bum rush every man within reach off the nearest cliff. He was avoiding me. And he was avoiding me because he was angry, of course. Angry I'd interfered. Angry, perhaps, I'd ruined his life.

But, a little optimistic voice inside me said, he hasn't left yet.

Be quiet, I told that little voice, or I'll squash you like Pinocchio squashed Jiminy Cricket.

"What I don't understand," Fox said, "is why you didn't pick a better costume this time. You had a second chance. And for the second time, Dashiell, you chose to be a cat that was beaten to death with a keyboard."

"Not my costume," I said. "Also, what is your costume?"

Fox gave me a scandalized look and then, with one arm, made a sweeping gesture to encompass their costume: a dirndl, welding gloves that went to the elbow, and tissue-paper butterfly wings that made it impossible for them to do anything but perch on the edge of the hassock. "I," Fox announced, "am a human being."

Keme and I rolled our eyes at the same time.

"I think your costume is very nice, Dash," Indira said. She'd gone for her tweed-and-deerstalker look, and she glanced over at me now as she filled paper cups with hot cider. "Kitty cats are very cute."

I hadn't been going for cute, not exactly. I mean, I wasn't West. I didn't have zero body fat and perfectly sculpted muscles. I certainly didn't have abs. But in a black tee and black jeans and black Chucks, with little black cat ears perched on my head, and for once in my life, my hair was actually doing a thing I could be proud of—well, I thought I looked good. The little keyboard letters CTRL + C glued to the front of my shirt were kind of like a safeguard. If I couldn't be hot, at least I could be clever, right?

But I didn't want to go into all that, so I settled for "Thank you, Indira."

Keme made a gagging noise, which immediately made Millie start giggling as she tried to shush him.

The doorbell rang, and Keme immediately recovered. But I was faster. I grabbed the pumpkin bowl and sprinted for the door, and he let out a wordless shout of outrage as he chased after me. He caught up with me as I started to open the door, and it turned into a wrestling match that resulted in a lot of laugh-shouts of protest (me), weirdly unnecessary teenage boy aggression (Keme), and a lot of mini Charleston Chews spilling onto the floor. Finally, Keme wrenched the bowl away from me, shouldered open the door, and held out the candy, breathing hard.

Deputy Bobby was standing there with a group of children. The kids were staring with huge eyes. Deputy Bobby looked like he was about to haul me and Keme in for disturbing the peace. He gave us a withering look, took the bowl from Keme, and said to the kids as he turned to them, "This is why some people, even adults, shouldn't eat too much candy. Here, everybody take two. Oh,

George, that is such an awesome chipmunk costume. Are you Alvin? And Emma, are you Wonder Woman? Don't get me with your lasso!"

Emma, the Wonder Woman in question, did some excited flailing with the lasso in question. If I hadn't been wearing my glasses, I probably would have lost an eye.

A few moments later, Deputy Bobby sent the kids back down the hill to their waiting parents. As little footsteps faded into the night, he straightened and turned back to me.

He was dressed in a blue uniform, with shiny black shoes that had to be incredibly uncomfortable and a peaked cap. It looked like a lot of polyester. It looked itchy. It looked like it had been packed in plastic and hanging on the pegboard at the Keel Haul General Store. The patch on the sleeve said HAPPY TOWN POLICE DEPARTMENT, and somehow, he'd gotten a little brass plaque for his shirt that said OFFICER BOBBY.

He was looking at me with a funny expression on his face, and I realized I was staring.

"Everything okay?" he asked.

I nodded and made myself say, "Hi, Officer Bobby."

(Yep. I totally nailed it.)

His mouth tilted into a smile, and he stretched up to flick the cat ears I was wearing. "Hello, Copy Cat."

I forgot about everything else. Literally everything else. Except, maybe, slightly, about how it felt when his hand brushed my hair. "Oh my God, you got it!"

"Well, it's not exactly hard—"

"Fox! I told you it was a good costume! Come on, you have to tell Fox."

It was strange how easy the night was after that. Hemlock House was warm and bright and safe. There was plenty of hot cider to drink, not to mention all that candy. Kids came, kids went. Keme ragged on Bobby for going as a police officer, and Bobby, laughing, tried to defend himself by explaining that a deputy and a police officer were two different things (which made all of us groan). And at some point during the night, in the midst of all that laughing and talking and Keme trying to convince me to arm-wrestle him, I realized I was happy, and Hemlock House had become home.

The trickle of kids slowed, and then it stopped all together. I left some candy on the terrace and locked the front door, and we moved into the billiard room. Somehow, Bobby and I ended up on a settee that was technically big enough for two people, although that was probably only true if one of those people was a fainting Victorian waif and the other was a fainting Victorian maiden. Bobby, so that we'd both be comfortable, stretched one arm out along the back of the settee. Which meant, technically, his arm was behind me. Almost around me.

"HOW?"

Here's a quick tip, totally free: cold showers? They've got nothing on Millie.

"HOW," Millie asked again, "HAVE YOU NEVER SEEN *HOCUS POCUS?*"

"I don't know," Keme said. "It's a kids' movie."

"Oh my God, no. I mean, it's about kids, yeah, but there's also this talking cat, and there's a zombie, oh, and there are WITCHES! It's the BEST!"

"What about *Scream*—"

"Don't be ridiculous," Indira said. "You'll have nightmares for a week."

The look on Keme's face was priceless.

"Nightmares," I said under my breath.

"Be nice," Bobby murmured in my ear.

"*Hocus Pocus* is great," Fox said. "Put it on."

That seemed to settle the matter for Keme (although, God knows, if I'd tried the same thing, he probably would have put on *The Texas Chainsaw Massacre* just to spite me). Millie, Fox, and Indira took the chesterfield, and Keme stretched out on the floor, and we started the movie.

Fox didn't last long; they kept making a suspicious noise, their head drooping, and then jolting upright. Indira finally offered to drive them home, which Fox accepted. Then Millie stretched out on the couch, and I entertained myself by watching Keme try to sneak glances at her until Bobby poked me in the ribs and gave me a look. Millie went next; after a period of silence that was far too long for her to have been conscious, she sat up groggily, explained she had to be at Chipper early the next morning, and headed out (shaking her head at Bobby's offer to make sure she got home safely).

Keme, meanwhile, had gotten glued to the screen.

"Why are they all so dumb?" he asked.

"We don't have to finish it," I told him.

"No, don't turn it off. Millie said they sing a song."

My eyebrows must have done some talking for me because Bobby whispered, "Let it go."

So, we watched the rest of the movie—if you can call it watching when you're hyperaware of the arm behind you and in a state of constantly escalating tension because he's here and he's right next to you, and oh my God every time he breathes you can feel his chest move against your shoulder.

When the movie ended, the credits rolled, and Keme's soft breathing blended with the music. Bobby and I sat there, in the quiet, in the dark. And maybe it was my imagination, but I thought I felt something building, an electric charge that kept bouncing from him to me to him to me, until it felt like I had a ball of lightning spinning in my stomach.

Bobby sat up and whispered, "I need my arm back."

"Oh. Sorry."

He squeezed my thigh in answer as he stood. When he crouched next to Keme, he whispered something, and Keme groaned in protest. Bobby whispered something else, and he helped Keme sit up, then stand, and a moment later, he was easing Keme down on the chesterfield.

By then, I'd recovered from my heart attack enough that I could get to my feet. (I could still feel where he'd touched my leg.) I found a blanket and unfolded it, and in the weak light from the television, Bobby helped me spread it over Keme, who was already asleep again. When we'd finished, Bobby was standing next to me, his shoulder brushing mine.

"You don't mind if he sleeps here?" Bobby whispered.

I shook my head. Then, realizing he might not be able to make out the movement in the dark, I whispered back, "No."

It felt like a long time before Bobby said, "I guess we should call it a night."

We made our way out of the billiard room, and I closed the pocket doors gently. We fought our way through Millie's spider webs (literally) and followed the stairs up to the second floor. We stopped. Bobby's room was to the right. My room was to the left. Neither of us turned.

"So," Bobby said, and he wore a strange half-smile, "I saw Damian today."

"What? Oh. Okay. Wait, why?"

But Bobby ignored the question. "He asked me for your number. I didn't know if you wanted me to give it to him."

I made some sort of noise that might, somewhere, have meant something to someone.

"I guess he's going to stick around for a while," Bobby said. "He likes cold-water surfing. He's got a free place to stay until someone figures out the legal mess of the camp." And then that half-smile was back again. "He's definitely interested in you. He's also the jealous type; he stared daggers at me until he decided I wasn't a threat."

The best I could come up with was that noise again.

"So, do you want me to give him your number?"

"Uh, I don't know." I managed to suppress a wince as I heard myself, but only barely. "The arrest record does worry me a little. Plus, I'm kind of in a weird place still. After Hugo, I mean. And…" I couldn't bring myself to look at him. "…stuff." Seconds ticked past on the grandfather clock, and I managed to add,

"Also, I have seriously bad judgment when it comes to men. Like, for a while, I even thought Damian might be the killer. He's good with cars. He cares about the surf camp. He's got some gray in his beard, but I think he wants to be a kid still, and he acted really strangely when he saw Gerry hitting on me."

"Because he's into you."

"Maybe. He seems like he wants to mess around, though, not like he wants something serious."

"Messing around can be fun, though." His face was like a mask. A mask of someone happy, someone trying to be happy. "I think you should go for it."

The hurt was so intense that all I could do was mumble, "Yeah, okay." Somehow, I even added, "I guess I'll think about it."

"Okay," Bobby said, but his tone was off. "Oh, I wanted you to know I can figure something out. A place to live, I mean. I don't want to overstay."

"Uh huh."

"I'll start looking tomorrow."

I nodded. I couldn't look at him because my eyes stung, and I was sure if I looked at him, I'd burst into tears.

"Okay," Bobby said again. Tick-tick-tock. And then, in that stranger's voice, "Goodnight."

His steps whispered away on the carpet.

I wiped my eyes, and the words burst out of me: "Are you mad at me?"

Over his shoulder, he asked, "What?"

"Are you mad? Are you angry at me? Because I—like, do you hate me now, or something?"

"What?" he asked again, but this time it was his real voice, Bobby's voice. He turned and came back. His breathing changed, which meant he must have seen the tear tracks, and he said, "What are you talking about? God, no. Why would I be mad at you?"

"Because—because it was none of my business, and I shouldn't have said anything, and I ruined your life."

Silence swallowed us.

And then Bobby laughed. It was an unsteady sound, unraveling at the edges, but it sounded genuine enough. "You didn't ruin my life. And I'm not angry with you. I wasn't thrilled with your grand plan to make yourself bait for a killer, but I'm not angry." He waited. And then he asked, "What's going on?"

"You've been avoiding me. And I get it: I should have kept my mouth shut, and it wasn't my place to say anything, and if I hadn't said anything, you and West would have worked everything out. And then, that night with Jen, you were there, and I thought—" What I'd thought was too embarrassing to say out loud, so I said, "And I know you're trying to be nice by not making a big deal out of it, but you quit your job, and you're moving, and I feel like I ruined everything."

That laugh came again, and this time, even through my distress, I recognized the quality in it: strain, as though some other emotion were buckled under it. "I guess you figured it all out."

I tried not to, but I could feel him waiting, and after a few seconds I had to look at him. In the hall's weak light, the burnished bronze of his eyes looked like candle flames.

"You," he said carefully, "have nothing to feel bad about. Do you understand?"

I didn't say anything.

"West and I." He stopped, and in the darkness, I could hear him swallow. "I should have done that a long time ago; it wasn't fair to anyone, letting it keep going like that. But I didn't know how. Or I wasn't brave enough. Or something. You helped me, Dash. I'll always be grateful for that. I'll always be grateful for you. You—" He stopped, and the moment hung for what felt like an eternity. Then a smile sliced across his face. "It feels like I don't know how to do anything anymore. How to—" He seemed to be searching my face for something. "How to say anything. How to tell you what I want to tell you."

And then another of those eternal moments came. His breath had a tremulous quality. And I remembered what he'd said, how hard this was for him, to try to say the things that mattered most, and the spinning, slicing fear that came with it. He'd told me, not so long ago, that he didn't feel that way with me. I wondered what had changed.

He still hadn't said anything, and I realized maybe he couldn't. Maybe this was one of those times I could do something for him.

So, I said, "Welcome to my life."

That jarred a laugh out of him, and I laughed too—weak laughs, meant more for each other, I thought, than anything else.

But when the laughter had faded, a hint of that big, goofy grin lingered on Bobby's face. "What about you?"

"What about me?"

"We had a deal, right? You were going to send off that story. I was going to write down my feelings and talk to West." He sounded like he was trying for lighthearted when he added, "I hope yours went better than mine did."

"Uh, yeah, actually. My dad emailed me back this morning. Honestly, I haven't really had time to think about it."

"God, Dash, that's great. I'm so proud of you."

Which shouldn't have made me feel the way it did, but I couldn't stop the idiot smile that spread across my face. "Yeah. Thanks."

"And?"

"And what?"

"Don't make me shake you."

A little laugh escaped me. "He said—well, he said it was great."

"Of course it was," Bobby said. He hesitated. "I haven't been avoiding you, by the way."

"Okay. That's good."

"I was getting my stuff out of the apartment before the movers came."

"Oh." I couldn't help asking, "So, West is..."

Bobby nodded.

"He called Indira and told us not to come," I said. "I thought maybe that meant he was staying."

"No."

"Where's your stuff?"

That made him laugh again. "In storage."

"Oh," I said again. Because my brain works good sometimes.

"And I didn't quit my job. The sheriff and I had a long talk."

"Wait, really? Bobby, that's amazing. God, that's wonderful. You're such a good deputy."

"I don't know about that. But the sheriff made some convincing points." His eyes crinkled. "Among other things, she suggested you might get yourself killed if I wasn't around to help."

"Okay, first of all, how dare you?"

That big, goofy grin bloomed in full, and for an instant, he was the old Bobby again. "So, that's that. I've got my job back. I'm not going anywhere. Everything I own is at the Park & Store. I am officially homeless. And most important, we're still friends."

"You're not homeless," I said. "You can stay here as long as you want."

His expression changed again, and once more I got the impression that he was searching my face for an answer to a question I hadn't heard. Something grew in the silence—grew and grew until it was a weight on my chest and I couldn't seem to draw a deep breath. That he might say something. Or that I might. Or that he might cross those last, final inches—

And then the moment passed, and he said, "Thanks. Maybe I'll take you up on that."

He didn't move. And neither did I. And that sense came again: of something building between us, something so big that there wasn't any room left for air.

The grandfather clock began to toll the hour, and whatever it had been, it was gone.

Bobby's crooked smile could have meant anything. "Goodnight, Dash."

"Goodnight, Bobby."

I didn't think about it; if I'd thought about it, I would have honestly, literally, instantly died. I leaned in and kissed his cheek. Just a brush of my lips, really. When I stepped back, my face was hot.

Bobby's hand rose like he wanted to touch his cheek, but he stopped himself at the last moment. His eyes were wide. And then, slowly, he grinned.

The clock was still tolling. Twelve chimes. Twelve hours. Midnight, I thought. And then, more clearly: It's a new day.

I caught Bobby's gaze, held it for a moment, and let a smile of my own slip out. And then I said, "Welcome home."

BROKEN BIRD

Keep reading for a sneak preview of *Broken Bird*, the next book in The Last Picks.

CHAPTER 1

"Where's Bobby?" I asked.

No one bothered to answer me, but that might have been because the library was so noisy. For a library, I mean—a low-grade roar of voices just begging to be shushed. Indira, Fox, Keme, Millie, and I took up a full row of seats in the multipurpose room, where it looked like pretty much the rest of the town had gathered. Say what you would about Hastings Rock (its shockingly high murder rate, for example), the people here loved books. Tonight, thriller-writer extraordinaire Marshall Crowe (author of the Chase Thunder series) was stopping in Hastings Rock to promote his latest book (*Thunder Clap*, book seventeen in the Chase Thunder series).

The library's multipurpose room was decked out for the occasion—well, for multiple occasions, which was probably the point of a multipurpose room. At the far end of the room was a temporary stage, complete with podium and chairs and an easel displaying a poster of Marshall Crowe's handsomely grizzled face. (Chase Thunder, by no coincidence, was also handsomely grizzled, and in literally every book of the series, yet another tall, striking, dark-haired, Amazon-esque woman fell prey to his charms—only to be abandoned when Chase Thunder inevitably moved on.)

But the library also had paper snowflakes hanging from the, admittedly, water-stained acoustic tiles, and it had glittery snowmen taped to the walls, and an enormous candy cane propped in the corner. (God only knew why they had it or what it could be used for—clubbing children over the head after they'd been lured inside a gingerbread house seemed like the only practical possibility.) Tinsel-strewn paper chains hung everywhere. With so many bodies crammed into such a small space, the smell of overheated synthetics mixed with aging bindings and carpet that needed to be torn up. Everyone seemed to be having a great time. Mr. Ratcliff was nosing around the stage, clearly hoping he'd pick up some interesting tidbit he could share with the rest of the town. Princess McAdams (not a real princess) had come dressed from head to toe in camouflage, and it looked like she'd brought the stock of a shotgun, presumably for Marshall to sign. And Mrs. Shufflebottom—librarian, wearer of vacuum-sealed cardigans, and apparently, for reasons unbeknownst to me, my self-appointed nemesis—was currently trying to force a family of six (tourists who had apparently wandered in during the off season) into the already overfull space. It was enough to make me, with my charmingly mild case of social anxiety, want to bite someone.

And still no Bobby. I checked my phone, but I hadn't missed any messages from him.

"Dash, aren't you so excited?"

Even over the hub of voices, Millie's carried.

"I'm excited to get out of here," I said. "Does anybody know where Bobby is?"

"He's probably running late, dear," Indira said.

"I know he's running late," I said. "I mean, he's not here yet, is he?"

Indira looked at me. The thing about Indira is that she's probably a good thirty years older than me, still strikingly handsome, utterly composed, and has a lock of white hair like a witch.

All of which were good reasons for me to mumble, "Sorry. It's all these people."

Keme snorted.

"But aren't you excited," Millie asked again, "to see your FRIEND?"

"He's not really my friend," I said.

"But you brought him a Christmas present," Millie said, looking at the parcel wrapped in brown paper (and string—that was my mom for you) under my chair.

"My parents sent that to my house. It's from my parents because my parents are friends with him." And this was true. My parents were both writers as well—my dad leaned toward military thrillers, not too different from Marshall's (Jonny Dane, the Talon Maverick series), and my mom wrote psychological thrillers (Patricia Lockley, *The Echoes in the Cellar, We All Live in the Basement, The Matriarch's Tooth*). And in addition to the parcel for Marshall, I'd gotten a package of my own from my parents—handwritten edits on my latest short story ("And Then They Were Done," and let me tell, my parents did *not* like the title). "He probably doesn't even remember me."

Although that, at least, definitely wasn't true. Because when I'd turned twelve, Marshall had happened to be visiting my parents, and he'd been kind enough to give me a BB gun—and then been crushed to learn I didn't want to go hunting with him and my dad. I hadn't been all that surprised when, a couple of books later in the Chase Thunder series, Chase had been saddled with a pansy twelve-year-old who didn't want to hunt, had zero self-confidence, oh, and ultimately got butchered in particularly disturbing detail. (To put your minds at rest, yes, Chase goes on to exact about two hundred pages of bloody revenge.)

In other words, I was really looking forward to seeing Marshall again. Which was part of why I looked around again. If nothing else, Bobby could shoot Marshall if he got particularly annoying. Not that Bobby would, because he was too kind. But maybe he'd let me borrow his gun.

But, as had become more and more often the case, there was no sign of Bobby. Things had certainly been different since he'd broken up with West and, with no place left to go, moved into Hemlock House. I wasn't sure what I'd expected—okay, I had some very clear hopes and dreams, and yes, maybe one of them involved a bubble bath. But I also understood that Bobby was just a friend, and as far as I could tell, that's all he wanted to be.

In fact, considering how things had gone lately, he might not even want *that*. He was hardly ever home, and when he was, he was busy, or the rest of the Last Picks were there, or he headed to his room. He went to the gym. He worked as many shifts as he could get at the sheriff's office. And slowly, over the last couple of months, I'd realized that I saw less of Bobby now that we were roommates than I ever had when he'd been engaged and living with his fiancé.

"I'm sure Marshall remembers you," Fox said. Tonight, they'd gone with corpse bride meets James Fennimore Cooper as their fashion choice: a striped, ruffled dress over buckskin leggings and clonky boots. "Who wouldn't remember you?"

"Uh, thank you?"

Keme and Fox both got a good laugh out of that.

I would have responded to that (probably), except raised voices drew my gaze.

At the back of the multipurpose room, my *other* self-appointed nemesis, Pippi Parker, was trying to clear people away from the coffee station. Pippi was yet another author—Hastings Rock was lousy with them, it turned out. She was a middle-aged white lady with platinum-colored hair in a pixie cut that looked like it had been blow-dried within an inch of catching fire. She wrote cozy mysteries. You know the type: everyone is friends, everyone gets along (well, except whoever got murdered, I suppose), calories don't count, and nobody says bad words, not even when Keme was hiding in your bedroom and he jumped out and screamed, and then you screamed, and then you had a minor heart attack, and Keme and Fox laughed so hard that Fox fell over and you had to take them to the urgent care because, according to them, the fall had made their sciatica flare up (painful and believable) and they needed their laudanum refilled (less believable).

Right then, Pippi was directing her family as they began unpacking the bags they were carrying. Accompanying Pippi tonight were her beloved husband Stephen, balding, in a reindeer sweater vest, and her three sons (their names were Dylan, Christian, and Carter, although I couldn't have told you which one was which; all three of them looked the same, with dishwater blond hair and obnoxiously friendly smiles, and they were all painfully polite and well-mannered). Under Mrs. Shufflebottom's approving gaze, Pippi's family was setting out what appeared to be an entire trade catalogue's worth of promotional materials: Pippi Parker-branded pens, Pippi Parker-branded keychains, Pippi Parker bookmarks (*Park Yourself with a Good Book!*), even Pippi Parker-branded cups, napkins, and—

"Good Lord," Fox said. "She has her own water bottles?"

Sure enough, a sticker with Pippi Parker's face had been pasted over the water bottle labels. All I could do was watch as Stephen hustled to the stage and started setting out the branded water bottles for Marshall and whoever else might end up sitting there.

"It does seem like a bit much," Indira said.

"I think it's a great idea," Millie said. "Dash, we should put your face on everything we drink."

"I think I've got a little more class—" I began to say.

And at that exact moment, of course, the room fell into one of those conversational lulls that occasionally happen.

"—than to slap my face on every available surface."

Every eye turned toward me as my words rang out through the multipurpose room.

Mrs. Shufflebottom recovered first, glaring at me, one hand pinching the cardigan shut at her throat. "Mr. Dane," she stage-whispered, "this is a library. If you cannot keep your voice down, I will have to ask you to leave."

Some bozo—I thought it sounded like one of the Archer clan—made a familiar, high school noise, the one that suggested: a) I'd gotten in trouble, and b) this was going to be good.

"But," I said, and I made a flailing gesture at the roomful of people who had chosen that particular instant to fall silent. I tried not to see Pippi's death stare. "Everyone was—I mean, I wasn't trying to—it was so loud in here—"

"Mr. Dane," Mrs. Shufflebottom snapped. And then, yanking the cardigan up a few inches: "Control yourself."

I sank down in my seat.

And then Millie waved. "HI, MRS. SHUFFLEBOTTOM."

A few of the people closest to us were knocked backward by the gale-force winds.

"Well, hello, Millicent," Mrs. Shufflebottom said, her voice changing to that syrupy sweetness I associated with librarians who spent too much of their lives doing story time. "Aren't you looking lovely this evening?"

To be fair, Millie was looking lovely this evening—you could tell by the fact that Keme practically fainted every time Millie said something to him—but the injustice of it still made me whisper, "How is that fair? I barely said anything—"

"Mr. Dane!"

I sank down even further and clamped my mouth shut.

Slowly, nervous chatter began, and the volume began to build again.

"She really doesn't like you," Fox informed me.

I glared at him.

Keme was smirking, so I gave him a dose too.

"What did you do to her?" Millie asked.

"I didn't do anything," I whispered furiously. "I've been nothing but charming and polite and charming and—"

"Polite?" Fox murmured.

While I tried to ratchet up the glare a few degrees, Indira said, "It's not your fault, Dashiell."

"Thank you."

"You're a lovely young man."

"Thank—wait, why does it sound bad when you say it like that?"

"I think you and Mrs. Shufflebottom just got off on the wrong foot," Millie said. "Because you came to town, and you killed Mrs. Shufflebottom's favorite author—"

"I didn't kill anyone!"

"—and then it turned out that you didn't kill her, but you exposed her as a murderer, and you destroyed her reputation, and you destroyed her legacy in Hastings Rock—well, her legacy all over the world, actually—"

"I didn't destroy anything!"

"—and then you spilled that hot chocolate all over her library books—"

"That was Keme's fault! What would you do if he jumped out of the closet at you and you were holding a nice, big mug of delicious hot chocolate?"

"—so Mrs. Shufflebottom probably just, you know, needs to get to know you."

"If she has a chance to get to know me," I said, "she'll probably bonk me with that candy cane and turn me into kidney pie."

"Oh no, Mrs. Shufflebottom is the SWEETEST. She did the best story times. I was always her favorite because I was the BEST at being QUIET!"

The excitement at the end meant a little ramp-up from ear-splitting to ear-shattering. Even Indira's eyes widened slightly.

Once again, I was spared having to respond. A wave of interested murmurs ran through the crowd, and I craned my head to see Marshall Crowe enter the multipurpose room. He hadn't changed much since the last time I'd seen him. He was tall and muscular, although at his age, muscular meant a built that leaned toward stocky. His hair was dark with presidential gray at the temples, and he wore a black military jacket over a black tee, with black jeans and black boots. I guessed black underwear was involved at some point, and I knew for a fact that he needed reading glasses. I was looking forward to when he had to pull out a pair of cheaters.

Behind him came two much younger people: a man and a woman. The woman was white, in her twenties, her mousy hair in a bun held by two pencils. Cardigan, cameo locket, pearl earrings, and dark pantyhose all suggested a Carter-era schoolmarm, but her face was alight with an excitement that made her look even younger. I pegged the man as close to my age, Black, his hair in twists. He was around my height, but muscular instead of, uh, whatever I was. (Slender. I should have said slender.) He wore a tweed blazer with a pocket square that, yes, somehow he actually pulled off, and he gave the general impression of a guy who owned a fedora (in a *GQ* way, not in a neckbeard way— did anybody still read *GQ*? Should *I* be reading it?)

"Who are they?" Millie whispered, which meant Mrs. Shufflebottom's head came up and whipped around, and I tried to use Fox as cover.

"I don't know," I said, "but I'm going to get this over with. Wish me luck."

"GOOD LUCK!"

I swear, one of the acoustic tiles shifted overhead.

A few of Hastings Rock's best and brightest hovered nearby, clearly waiting for a chance to approach Marshall. I wasn't sure they were going to get it—as I watched, Marshall looked up from his conversation with the young woman who'd accompanied him and scowled at JaDonna Powers (church hair) as she made an approach. JaDonna swerved left, her face flushed as she scurried back to her seat.

I was jealous; I would have loved to scurry back to my seat. To scurry back to Hemlock House, as a matter of fact. But if I didn't give Marshall his parcel now, I'd have to find an opportunity to do it later, and that would probably mean drinks, and a meal, and more drinks—and I could see the evening getting longer and longer. And why would any sensible person spend all that time in a bar or a restaurant, around other people, when they could be safely at home, in their pajamas, on the couch, watching, for the fourteenth time, season two of *Supernatural*? (With no one talking to them.)

So, I crossed the no-man's-land of open floor between the crowd and Marshall. Marshall hadn't noticed me yet, his head bent as he whispered furiously to the woman who had arrived with him. As I got closer, I caught the tail end of his words.

"—don't know why you're acting like this," Marshall said. "Anybody else would feel lucky to be in your position."

The woman opened her mouth, and then she saw me. Something in her expression must have alerted Marshall because he turned. He didn't recognize me. And then he did, and he pasted on a smile as he roared, "Killer!"

Egad. I'd forgotten about that stupid nickname.

Before I could recover, Marshall wrapped me in a bear hug. Then, with a shake, he released me. "Well—" And then Marshall chose to use several colorful expressions favored by Chase Thunder, which weren't really fit for public consumption. "I was wondering when you'd pop your head up. Where's Hubert?"

"Hugo," I said. "And we broke up. That's why I'm here, as I'm sure my parents told you. Dramatic flight across the country. Total mental and emotional breakdown. I have a pet seal now who makes all my financial decisions."

I don't know why I threw in the pet seal thing; to get a rise out of him, I guess. As usual, though, Marshall ignored it. He said another of Chase Thunder's favorite words, and then "Really? That's too bad; I liked him."

"Not enough to remember his name."

He gave me a considering look, and I realized the Dash of a few years ago—heck, the Dash of *last* year—wouldn't have said something like that. But then Marshall just grinned again and said, in a different tone, "Killer." He reached out like he might scrub his hand through my hair—or, God, give me noogies—and I managed a dodge. The movement was uncoordinated, and I caught a whiff of his breath, and with a flash of surprise, I realized Marshall had been drinking. I gave him another, closer look—the slight slackness to his face, the cloudy eyes—and upgraded that to *drunk*.

Instead of trying again, though, Marshall only said, "How's the writing going? I saw that gay thing."

That gay thing (which was now how I was going to refer to it) was a story that I'd had published at an online crime fiction magazine called *The Midnight Messenger*. I had a feeling that Marshall and people of his generation looked down on e-zines because they weren't print, but *The Midnight Messenger* paid pro rates, and even better, they were actively searching for diverse authors. One of the editors had reached out to me about a last-minute story, after they had problems with another author, and—miracle of miracles—I managed to get "Pickup at Pershing" completed and sent off. Even better, it wasn't a Will Gower story; I'd tried something new. Granted, I'd only finished it and sent it off because Keme had hidden the Xbox and Millie had brought me a million coffees and Fox had threatened to give me a "new" haircut and Indira had suggested the possibility of locking me in my room. And, of course, because Bobby had been so genuinely excited for me, and I honestly couldn't stand the thought of disappointing him.

"God," Marshall said before I had a chance to speak, "that's got to have Chandler spinning in his grave."

"He'll survive," I said. "Or not, I guess. I love Chandler's stories and what he did for crime fiction, but he was a massive homophobe. There's a ton of homophobia baked into the crime fiction genre, actually. I think it's time to start pushing back on that, don't you?"

Marshall gave me that considering look again and grunted; I didn't think I'd be reading an impassioned speech from Chase Thunder about the importance of gay rights anytime soon, but Marshall didn't argue. (Which was a good thing: my knees had reached melted-butter status, and I was so sweaty I thought I was going to slide out of my shirt.)

"This is Elodie, my assistant," he said, jerking a thumb at the young woman. "She wants to be a writer. Like you. And that's Hayes, my agent." He must have meant the guy who had come in with him, but before I could check, he continued, "Elodie, work something out for Dash—dinner and drinks after."

"I really can't—" I tried, and I used all my mental energy to visualize a night of nachos, then Indira's cookies, and then the episode of *Supernatural* when John—well, I don't want to give anything away.

"Nonsense. We'll call your parents; they'll be thrilled."

With that, Marshall headed toward the stage.

The worst part was, he was right: my parents *would* be thrilled. And it would be awful.

"It's so nice to meet you," Elodie said. Her voice was high and excited, and any trace of the argument—or whatever it had been—was gone. "I met your parents a few months ago, and they were so lovely!"

"Thank you," I said. "I guess I should give you this—"

As I held out the parcel, though, another hand seized it before Elodie could take it. Marshall gripped the package a little too tightly, his hand tense, his fingers dimpling the paper. "I'll take that," he said. "I forgot they were sending it here. Thanks for being the mailman, Killer."

And then he hurried toward the stage.

"Now, about tonight," Elodie said, tapping her phone's screen so quickly that her fingers seemed to blur. "We had drinks at a great microbrewery last night, but I understand there are a few local bars. You're the expert; would you like to pick?"

"Let me think about it," I said. "There are so many good options. Can I tell you after the reading?"

Elodie burbled an enthusiastic yes, and I retreated to my seat.

That, ladies and gentlemen, is called *thinking on your feet* and *seizing an opportunity*.

"Dash, that was amazing," Millie said. "You're FAMOUS!"

"I'm not—"

"Did you talk about writing? Did he tell you you're a good writer? Did you tell him it's hard for you to write sometimes? OH! Did you tell him about your special meditation with your eyes closed and sometimes you have to put a pillow over your face?"

Don't judge. Sometimes a guy just needs a nap, and his wonderful, loving, well-meaning friends won't. leave him. alone.

"Special meditation," Fox said scornfully.

"I went by your studio last week," I told them. "You were taking a nap on the floor behind the counter. The door wasn't even locked."

"That," Fox said, doubling down on the scorn, "was different."

"How?"

"Tell him, Keme."

Keme gave each of us a long, withering stare.

"He doesn't seem like a very happy man," Indira said. And then, almost as a question to me, "But maybe he's different when you get to know him."

"No, that's pretty much how he always is."

"Is he always snookered?" Fox asked.

"Fox," Indira said.

"Look at him; he can barely stand up straight."

Up onstage, Marshall did look a little…wobbly. He was drinking some of the Pippi water (God, it sounds so bad when I say it out loud)—he was drinking some of the water with Pippi's face stuck to the bottle, and he was staring out into the distance, his eyes glassy. A moment later, Pippi joined him on stage. In contrast, she looked all aquiver for the event—and, just possibly, like she'd found a hot minute to duck into the restroom and volumize her hair one more time. Mrs. Shufflebottom joined them, and she spoke first to Pippi and then to Marshall. Pippi took one of the chairs. Marshall didn't, and it was clear, from how Mrs. Shufflebottom waited, that she didn't know what to do. After another moment, Pippi stood.

"Is this how authors are supposed to act?" Millie asked me.

"Neurotic and awkward and crippled by self-doubt?" I said. "That's kind of the baseline."

"We artists suffer for our art," Fox said. "That's why I need a Ring Ding."

"There aren't any Ring Dings," I said. "They have these chocolate imitation things that are supposed to be like Ho-Hos. They aren't bad, actually."

And of course, at that moment, Mrs. Shufflebottom approached the podium, and the room went silent, which meant everyone heard my opinion of the imitation chocolate cakes, or whatever they were called.

"If everyone is finished," Mrs. Shufflebottom said crisply into the microphone.

"I want to catch one break," I said under my breath. "Just one."

"Mr. Dane?"

I mimed zipping my lips.

"You really got under her skin," Fox murmured.

Opening my mouth seemed like asking for more trouble, so I settled for a glare.

With a final, pointed look for the troublemakers in the crowd (i.e., me), Mrs. Shufflebottom cleared her throat and said, "Welcome, everyone, to the Hastings Rock Public Library. This evening, we're thrilled to have two bestselling authors joining us to read from their latest releases. Many of you know Marshall Crowe from his bestselling Chase Thunder series. Mr. Crowe has hit every bestseller list you can name, and his popularity only continues to grow with the release of the latest entry in this series: *Thunder Clap*.

"We're also so pleased and grateful that one of our own could be here. I don't have to introduce Pippi Parker to anyone from Hastings Rock—"

"You might remember me," Pippi put in from behind Mrs. Shufflebottom, "from the Hastings High bake sales."

For some reason, that made everyone laugh. Even Mrs. Shufflebottom.

"She's been running them for years," Indira whispered. "She's an absolute tyrant. Won't let me donate anything."

"It's not fair," I whispered back. "If I chimed in like that, Mrs. Shufflebottom would have eviscerated me."

Maybe Mrs. Shufflebottom heard me, because she gave me a steely-eyed look like she was considering some eviscerating right then. After a brief summary of Pippi's own performance on the bestseller charts—which, Mrs. Shufflebottom was too polite to point out, had dropped off significantly in the last few years—Mrs. Shufflebottom announced, "And, of course, it comes as no surprise to anyone in Hastings Rock to hear that Pippi will be reading from her latest entry in the Aunt Lulu's Laundromat series, *Spin Cycle Secrets.*"

"It comes as a surprise to me," I whispered to Fox, who was trying to ignore me. "I thought that got canceled after everyone found out she'd hired Vivienne to do some ghost-writing."

"You mean after you revealed to everyone," Fox corrected—unnecessarily, in my opinion.

"Dash." It was a Millie-whisper. "Dash. DASH!"

My "What?" sounded, admittedly, a bit strangled.

"Why didn't they invite you to be in the reading?"

"Without further ado," Mrs. Shufflebottom said, "let's give a warm welcome to Mr. Crowe."

I sank back into my seat—grateful for a chance to dodge Millie's question—as Marshall approached the podium. Even though it was only a short distance, his steps were so unsteady that it looked more like a semi-controlled lurch, and he clutched the podium to steady himself. He bent too close to the microphone and spoke too loudly, and the slight scrape of feedback raised the hairs on the back of my neck.

"It's a pleasure to be here," he said, and the words had the blurred edges of someone losing his grip. "Wonderful town. Charming town. You know, most places you go, they're grateful to have a celebrity visit them. They feel lucky. They don't try to shoehorn in a housewife with an overactive imagination."

It was like an old sci-fi show when someone depressurized the airlock. I could almost hear the hiss. Pippi's face went pale, and then bright spots of color rose in her cheeks.

"I'm joking, I'm joking," Marshall said. "It's a real privilege to spend twelve hours traveling and end up sitting next to someone whose last book didn't sell enough copies to pay for a cup of coffee. Have you read—" He reached for the mic, and when it touched it, feedback screeched. He fumbled with the mic for a moment, and when the feedback stopped, he said, "Have you read her stuff? It's great. It's really inspiring. You don't see people like that anymore—people who don't let zero talent and even less common sense stop them."

Around me, the audience seemed to have gotten over their shock and was beginning to react. I remembered, when I'd first arrived in Hastings Rock, how many people had come to Pippi's reading. People had turned out in droves, and they'd come with bags of books for her to sign—and tonight was no exception. Althea and Bliss Wilson, off to one side of the room, shifted in their seats, murmuring their disapproval. Cyd Wofford was clutching a well-read copy of *Tumble Trouble*, his jaw set. A little farther down our row, Mr. Cheek, in a zebra-stripe blazer and patent leather heels, bared his teeth at Marshall and hissed his displeasure. Mrs. Shufflebottom, for her part, stood at the edge of the stage, clutching her cardigan at her throat, her face so white I thought she might faint.

"He's going to start a riot," Indira murmured.

"Why is he being so mean?" Millie asked.

Pippi, for her part, wore a rigid, meaningless smile. I remembered, the last time I'd been at one of her readings, how quick she'd been on her feet. She certainly hadn't been at a loss for things to say, and so it seemed strange for her to sit there, weathering Marshall's abuse. My only guess was that she still thought—hoped—he was joking, and if she played along, a good relationship with Marshall might outweigh the humiliation. Her husband, on the other hand, looked furious—from my interactions with Stephen, I'd always thought he had as much personality as sofa stuffing, which was probably a good balance to Pippi's more over-the-top persona. Right then, though, his face was red, his hands were curled into his fists, and he seemed to be having trouble breathing.

"Have ever read one of her books?" Marshall asked again with that leaden delivery. "You know what happens when you're a middle-aged housewife with no life experience trying to write a book? You write book after book about middle-aged housewives with no life experience. It doesn't matter how you dress them up; they're all the same. You know what I mean. She's got all these twenty-year-old cupcake bakers and booksellers and teahouse owners, but they don't talk like twenty-year-olds, they don't act like twenty-year-olds. They say things like 'Oh my,' and 'Golly.' They don't message each other—they don't even text. They call. When was the last time someone under thirty voluntarily made a phone call?"

Fox made a strange sound that it took me an instant to recognize as a laugh. I mean, I did still make phone calls, and I was under thirty, but I did prefer to text—and that's pretty much all Keme and Millie did—but Fox and Indira, who were both at least twenty years older than me, almost always called.

"Mr. Crowe," Mrs. Shufflebottom began in a quavering voice. "I'm going to have to insist—"

"And when they do call, do you know what they do?" Marshall swayed and caught the podium again to keep from going over. "They use a landline." He stopped like he might laugh, but he only blinked owlishly out at the audience. "The one I read, it was set in 2015, and every other chapter they're running home to check their voicemail."

A boo erupted from the crowd. I twisted and spotted the lumberjack—I didn't know his name, but I thought of him as Fox's lumberjack, since they had an ongoing, and apparently messy, quasi-relationship. Then I caught a glimpse of Marshall's assistant, Elodie. She must have realized that her boss had gone too far—she was pale, and I thought, for a moment, she looked like she might pass out. Then Mrs. Knight stood and booed as well, shaking a paperback of *Death by Dryer* at Marshall.

"You ought to be ashamed of yourself," Althea called from her seat.

Mr. Cheek hissed again and held up his hands like claws.

"A riot might have been underselling it," I said. "He's going to get himself killed. Keme, let's get everybody out of here—"

But before I could finish, the guy who had arrived with Marshall jogged down the center aisle. His face was fixed in what looked like polite goodwill, and he seemed to be trying not to make eye contact with any of the angry townspeople. As he approached the stage, he said in a low voice, "Hey, Marshall, why don't we take a break? You look like you're not feeling so hot."

Marshall didn't answer, but he did look worse than ever. His skin looked gray, his lips were tinged with blue, and his eyes looked bruised and sunken. His head bobbed, as though he were listening to music the rest of us couldn't hear.

The guy hopped up onto the stage and, as he rose, caught Marshall's arm. "Why don't we get some fresh air?"

Marshall twisted away, breaking the man's hold, and then planted a hand on the guy's chest and shoved. The guy fell backward off the stage and hit the floor hard enough that the thud carried over the audience's angry shouts.

"Come on," I said, touching Fox's shoulder. "This is getting out of control—"

But before I could finish, Marshall's eyes rolled up in his head, and he collapsed.

Silence dropped over the crowd. Everyone froze.

The guy who had been shoved from the stage picked himself up at the same time that I started toward Marshall.

"We need a doctor," I called. I caught Mrs. Shufflebottom's eye and said, "Call 911."

I reached Marshall at the same time as the guy he'd shoved off the stage. Marshall wasn't breathing, and when I tried to find a pulse, his skin was clammy.

Dr. Xu dropped onto her knees next to me a moment later. "Move back," she said as she leaned over Marshall.

But a part of me knew that, no matter what she tried, it wouldn't be enough. Because Marshall was dead.

ACKNOWLEDGEMENTS

My deepest thanks go out to the following people (in alphabetical order):

Jolanta Benal, for her help proofing this manuscript, in the process teaching me that "comprised of" is not actually correct (I had no idea!), and for her excellent question about the blackmail files.

Savannah Cordle, for her tremendously insightful observations about Bobby (and how Dash sees Bobby), for her thoughts about the first chapter and the info dump, and for taking the time to share her thoughts and notes about all the wackiness these people get up to.

Winston Eisiminger, for suggesting I consider whether these books could be read as standalones, for identifying points for clarity and readability (plus the great idea of a virtual assistant called Sherpa!), and for reminding me about battery vs. assault.

Austin Gwin, for helping me with continuity (about Gerry and Fox), accuracy (trifle! the inflatable tube man!), and for the incisive observation about Dash and the potential for a trans character.

Marie Lenglet, for such close attention to the text, helping me iron out continuity errors, strengthening the prose, and making everything with the mystery and relationship tighter and more powerful.

Raj Mangat, for pointing out inconsistencies in Bobby's behavior (some of which I hope I've addressed, and others which have stayed), for catching typos that slipped past everyone else, and for remembering the eight-cheese pasta!

Cheryl Oakley, for her help with my repetitions (Gerry's beard!), for asking me to explain more about how Dash solved the mystery, and for questioning how Bobby knew about the secret passage.

Meredith Otto, for pointing out that Dash can wax poetic about almost everything except Indira's hair, for asking about the name "Deputy Bobby," and for urging me to be more specific at key moments.

Pepe, for his excellent idea about Millie's spider webs at the end, for his corrections to the text, and for his question about Dash and Jen and the alternator at the end—which, unfortunately, I've left unasked.

Alicia Ramos, for help with repetition, repetition, repetition—oops. And for help with repetition. (Okay, and with so much else!)

Nichole Reeder, for lending her editorial eye to the prose, for all her help with the continuity, and for her excellent question about Damian at the end.

Mark Wallace, for catching those missing end marks, for helping me with my Hail Marys, and for lending his reader brain—with his insight into character-driven stories vs procedural mysteries.

Tray Stephenson, for helping me with my sport coat (s optional), for spotting my weird glitch with the coffee, and for his patience with an ending that didn't actually resolve all that much.

And special thanks to Alyssa, Brett, Crystal, Kathleen, and Raye for catching errors in the ARC (and Alyssa, in the acknowledgments!!).

About the Author

For advanced access, exclusive content, limited-time promotions, and insider information, please sign up for my mailing list at **www.gregoryashe.com**.

Made in the USA
Monee, IL
28 September 2024

66543865R00118